The Home Wind

Terri Martin

Gnarly Woods Publications
L'Anse, MI

© 2021 Gnarly Woods Publications

ISBN: 978-1-7352043-1-4

Library of Congress Control Number: 2021906337

First Edition 2021

10   9   8   7   6   5   4   3   2   1

Published by Gnarly Woods Publications
L'Anse, Michigan 49946

Cover art by Elizabeth Yelland

THE HOME WIND

*Gaa wiin daa aangoshkigaazo ahaw
enaabiyaan gaa inaabid*

You cannot destroy one who has dreamed a
dream like mine. (Ojibwa saying)

CONTENTS

PROLOGUE
April 27, 1870

"Close the sluice gate!" Jamie could barely hear his father's shouts above the booming rush of the river. The water and logs exploded with a thunderous roar through the sluice gate that Jamie and a riverman named Pete struggled to slide closed. But it was stuck. Jamie, pushing with the full might of his twelve-year old body, was unable to budge his side of the gate.

"She's gonna jam again," Jamie's father shouted from below as he fought his way along the bobbing and tumbling logs. The calks of his boots dug into bark, sending each log he stepped on into a spin before he leapt to another.

"Close the gate!" he shouted again.

But the water kept coming, its raging torrent carrying more giant logs through the sluiceway. Pete pushed Jamie aside and wrestled with the gate, but strong as Pete was, it was too much for one man. It was wedged tight at an angle because Jamie's end had not gone down.

Jamie balanced on the dam, surrounded by the foaming boil of angry water and timber. Pete was cussing, his voice mixing with the pounding water. Jamie's father was running across the unsteady bridge of logs, barely escaping disaster with each step.

"Lord in heaven, give me strength. Come back and help me, lad," Pete shouted.

1

The Home Wind

But Jamie stood paralyzed, as if his feet were nailed to the primitive dam structure. With unblinking eyes, he watched his father leaping from log to log. He could hear his father's cries for help, even though he was much too far away and the river's fury much too loud for any man's voice to carry.

Jamie's father was twenty feet from shore when he stumbled.

"Help me boy!" Pete screamed. "Lord, he's going down. Hell and damnation! It's too late."

His father balanced briefly on his hands and knees then pitched headfirst into the crush of water and logs.

"Pa?" Jamie stared at the place where his father had been.

Pete rushed across the dam to shore. He grabbed a peavey stick and sprinted along the bank down river, looking for his doomed comrade. Jamie, still glued to the dam, strained to watch, to hear. Pete raced around the bend, leaving Jamie to stare at the jam of logs which snagged and stacked haphazardly into a groaning mountain.

His pa had told him that the white pine had a spirit. It may only be a tree standing helpless as the lumberjacks slash their paths through the forests of Michigan with their axes and crosscut saws, but the spirit of a felled tree lives on, waiting to claim the life of a lumberjack.

PART ONE

FOX RIVER LOGGING CAMP

CHAPTER ONE
The Sluice Gate

Jamie.

He heard his pa's voice, ghostly—a spirit, calling.

Jamie!

I'm coming Father. I can't close the sluice gate, but I'm coming. Jamie watched the swirling vortex of water below him pounding against the jumble of logs. He felt his father's spirit pulling him into the fierce rapids of the river.

"James Kangas, rise and shine."

He could smell boiling coffee and the yeasty aroma of fresh-baked bread.

"Get up and wash your hands and face."

His ma's voice. Jamie opened his eyes a slit. He made out her silhouette in the dim kerosene light. She was still clad in widow's black, as it had not yet been a year since the accident.

"Men will be in for breakfast. Get going, James, and set the table."

Jamie sat up and stretched. His head throbbed and his legs were wobbly as he slid out of bed.

His ma cast a concerned look at him. "You're not feeling poorly are you James?"

"No, Ma. Just a little stove up."

"No wonder, all that running and fetching you do all day for the men."

The Home Wind

Jamie pulled his trousers and flannel shirt over his long johns. He shuffled his way to a pitcher perched on a stand and poured frigid water into a basin. He cupped his hands, scooped, and quickly splashed his face. The icy rivulets trickled down his neck and soaked his shirt. He shuddered.

"Hot water right here on the stove, son."

"Like it cold," muttered Jamie as he scrubbed his face with a piece of sacking. Truth was, he preferred hot, but Larry Flannigan had told him cold water would grow whiskers. Jamie was hoping for some sprouts before the end of winter. He couldn't wait to boast the tangled beard sported by nearly all the lumberjacks—sometimes called jacks for short. He'd let the snuff he spat freeze in it too, like the men.

Jamie collected the cutlery and tin plates and cups and distributed them across a long, rough-hewn table. He felt his body going through the motions of his morning routine, but his mind was still at the river, the angry roar rising and drowning out the clink of plates and the hiss of flapjacks cooking on the stove.

If he'd been a man instead of a boy… It was a job for two stout men, not a job for a lad with arms like willow sticks.

"Jamie, help me."

Pete and Jamie's father had gone to open the sluice gate to start the spring drive. Jamie had come only to watch. But it all went wrong.

"Jamie!"

He snapped around. His ma stood watching him, tapping her foot.

"Yes, Ma'am?"

"Where were you, James? Looked like a hundred miles away."

Jamie shrugged.

"Ring the dinner bell then help me with the bowls."

Jamie stepped outside the mess hall and grabbed the leather thong that hung from the dinner bell clapper. A few sharp rings would bring the men for breakfast. Jamie went back inside and carried steaming bowls of beans and deer meat to the table. He heard the sounds of feet outside the mess hall door as the men stomped snow from their boots. The lumberjacks were coming—over thirty of them—each with an insatiable appetite.

"Hey boy," shouted one jack, "that should do for me. What you gonna feed the rest of these fellas?"

Jamie heard his ma laugh as she marched up to the table and slapped down two heaping platters of hot flapjacks.

"Now, you gents sit your hides down and hush," she said with mock scolding. "No talking at my table."

The jacks knew she ruled her cook shack with an iron fist and muttered, "yes, Missus" and "right away, Ma'am." Woe be to any man who showed up unwashed or forgot to remove his hat at her table. He was certain to be sent away to scrub up and find scant offerings by the time he could hurry back. Or in the case of a forgotten "sky piece," the culprit's hat would be snatched from his head by a disgusted Mrs. Kangas and his ears lightly boxed. Those who bowed their heads in a moment of silent grace were sure to gain the favor of the Widow Kangas. She'd see to it that his flaggin's—his meal in the woods—was a little heartier than that of the heathen who simply dove into his grub without a word of thanks to his Maker. But as the foreman, Tom Haskins, had said, Anja Kangas whipped up the best chow this side of heaven and that made her more valuable than any sawyer or riverman. Any improprieties toward Jamie's ma were met with immediate dismissal from the employment of the Chicago Lumber Company.

Jamie was another story. As chore boy he had the dubious honor of holding the lowest station in the logging camp and all for the paltry wages of a dollar fifty per week. Jamie was run ragged the next half hour bringing more platters and bowls of food and pouring gallons of coffee for the men. Next came the pies, still warm from the ovens, sliced into thick wedges and greedily devoured. There was no talking while the men ate, only the sound of utensils clinking and utterings of appreciation: "Fine eatin' Missus. Chuck's better'n the pay, that's for sure." At the end of the meal, the jacks rose from the table and filed out of the mess hall to begin their day's work.

Only then did Jamie and his ma sit at the little table by the stove to eat their stack of flapjacks held back and kept warm under a towel. Next, Jamie helped his ma collect and scrape the plates, then wash the dishes in the tub full of steaming water. Some camp cooks didn't bother with the washing, but Jamie's ma lectured it was inviting disease to live in filth. The dishes done and stacked on their shelves, it was time for Jamie to start his day as chore boy, running to and fro with messages and food and, much more to his liking, helping the teamsters with their fine teams of horses.

Already his ma was cutting thick slices of bread and meat in preparation of the mid-day meal. She pulled a time piece from her apron pocket and studied it.

"Not bad, James, got breakfast behind us, and it's nary five thirty. Dawn should come soon. Getting light out earlier with spring coming."

Jamie nodded as he pulled his Mackinaw coat and wool hat off the peg next to his bed.

"Remember your schooling," she said, slipping the watch back into her apron.

"Yes Ma'am," Jamie said. He was required to spend an hour each afternoon, when light was best, practicing his ciphering and spelling and reading Bible verse.

Jamie slipped out into the snowy woods and headed for the stable to help with the harnessing. In twelve hours, it would be dark again. Then, after supper dishes, he would crawl under a pile of wool blankets onto his straw-stuffed mattress. Exhausted, he would soon sleep and the dream would torment him again. Only this time it would be different. This time he would dream of the man, James Kangas who, singlehandedly, would close the sluice gate.

CHAPTER TWO
An Eye For An Eye

The pleasant aroma of his ma's cooking was soon replaced by the pungent odor of the stable. Jamie didn't mind, though. He liked the horses and the smells and noises associated with them: The nickering and occasional impatient stamping of a hoof at feeding time and the popping noises their lips made when they skimmed hay chaff from the manger. The crude stable held twelve horses, or six teams. Three men worked the horses, each responsible for two teams, which they rotated. Jamie admired the gentleness of the burly teamsters as they coaxed and sweet-talked their charges through the day's work. And hard work it was for the beasts straining against their collars, pulling the skids from the forest to the riverbank where the logs were stacked. Jamie often watched in awe as a lumberjack sky-hooked the logs into an impossibly high pyramid on the skid.

It was the job of a chore boy to help where help was needed.

"Come here, boy, and untangle these traces," hollered one of the men.

"Hold Molly still, will you, son!" shouted another.

Jamie rushed about in a frenzy helping with buckles, adjusting bridles, and steadying the horses as they were harnessed.

The Home Wind

"Say, Jamie, I think Max has a loose shoe. Lift up his rear right hoof for me while I get a crimper. Mind you don't let that hoof down 'til I say. Horse moves just right, he'll cut himself with that loose shoe."

Jamie hurried to obey the teamster, Larry Flannigan. Jamie bent and lifted the hoof in question, squinting at the studded shoe. He tried to wriggle the shoe but it didn't budge. Well, Jamie thought, Flannigan knows what he's doing. He wondered, though, why it was taking so long to fetch a crimper. The smithy's shed was just through the door. Jamie's back soon began to protest and the horse, Max, who never missed an opportunity to rest, shifted a goodly portion of his bulk onto the boy. Soon Jamie's legs ached along with his neck and his arms were going numb with the strain.

"Where you 'spose Mr. Flannigan got to?" Jamie asked. But the other men were moving their teams out the doors into the dim light of the dawn.

"Mr. Flannigan?"

Well, he'd show them that he was no slacker. He'd hold this hoof until spring thaw if need be. Jamie shifted his position, moving from the side of Max's rear end directly under his tail. There, that was better.

Jamie felt a subtle shift in the horse as he lifted his tail. Before he could react, he felt the warmth and smelled the distinct aroma of manure as it plopped on the back of his neck.

"Hell and damnation!" he shouted. Ma forbid him to cuss, but it just slipped out. He dropped the hoof with a thud and tried to wipe himself clean with a handful of straw. Jamie nearly gagged up his breakfast when he felt a ball of the stuff work its way down his neck. Ma would be furious! She would make him launder his clothes and he would have no choice but to submit to an all-over scrubbing, ahead of the normal springtime ritual.

Larry Flannigan silhouetted the doorway, hands on hips, legs spread, and head thrown back with a roar of laughter. Max whinnied, a horse's laugh if Jamie ever heard one. Some of the jacks came around to see what the ruckus was and joined in the sport.

"Got you with the loose shoe prank, huh boy? You really thought you had to hold up that hoof just 'cause the shoe was loose?"

"C'mere, will ya? I gotta pair of socks you need to hold up 'til they dry. Don't let'em touch the ground now lad, or you'll have to wash them and start all over. Har har!"

Jamie felt his checks flush. He stripped off his shirt, making further spectacle of himself by exposing his runty torso. This brought more jeers and rude comments from the men. Finally, freeing his clothing of the manure, he re-dressed and pushed past his tormentors through the door.

Jamie's cheeks, laced with tears, stung in the cold air. He took refuge in the privy, sitting over the hole with his drawers still up. In spite of the cold, the blended odors of the privy and the horse manure were strong and again Jamie fought to keep his breakfast down. He hunched in a ball clutching his knees and wept. Tears dropped and froze to the scarred floor.

"Jamie lad."

Somebody was rapping on the door.

"Go away," Jamie said. "I'm busy."

"Now come on James. The men were only having some fun. Come on out of there 'fore you choke on the fumes."

Jamie recognized the voice. It was Pete Atkins, the riverman on the sluice gate. He was also a teamster in the winter.

"Just leave me alone." Jamie hated the sound of his shrill, boyish voice.

"Now, son, fellas wouldn't tease ya so if they didn't like ya."

Jamie mulled on this for a while. He uncoiled his body and reached to crack the door. "Don't make sense to me," Jamie said through the door slit. "Somebody likes a body, why would they cause him misery?"

"Because they're a bunch of hooligans, that's why. Don't know any better. Way I see it, best thing to do is show them how much you like them—so to speak."

"Right now, I don't like 'em much." Jamie stood and slipped out of the privy into the fresh air. He took a deep, ragged breath. "Course, I don't hate 'em or anything."

"Naw, not Christian-like to hate. But the Lord wouldn't mind a little of that eye for an eye, tooth for a tooth thing."

Jamie had read that Bible passage. He had also heard about turning the other cheek. It was a little confusing, but he expected it depended on the situation. Right now the eye for an eye suited him. He'd like to thrash Larry Flannigan then and there, make him bleed. But Jamie knew the powerful Flannigan, famous for his brawling, would squash him like an overripe grape.

Pete put his arm around Jamie's shoulders and they walked back to the stable. Jamie's next task of the day was to muck out the barn and brush the teams who were enjoying their day off. Maybe he could tell his ma that he had aimed badly with a pitchfork and got some droppings down his shirt. It would be a fib but that was probably better than betraying the jacks by telling the truth. That would be breaking the code of a lumberjack.

"Now listen here boy, you get to thinkin' about this and let me know if I can help. I owe Flannigan one or two myself."

Jamie nodded and cracked a smile.

Pete smiled back and headed out the door. He hesitated and turned around, his mouth opening as if to say something. Jamie waited, expectantly.

"You reckon your ma will be making up deer meat sandwiches for our flaggin's?'

"No, sir, I think it's gonna be ham slabs and butter today. Baked the bread fresh this morning. Got some canned peaches, too. 'course may not be enough to go around of the peaches."

Pete nodded. "I'll be in the north quarter, sprinkling. Why don't you ride the Swede out today? He could use the exercise."

Jamie felt his heart lighten. The Swede was half of Pete's second team. Ride the Swede!

He was a grand horse with a dun coat and black points. Most of the horses were ordinary brown or black. Swede's harness mate, Viking, had come up lame, and the Swede had not been under harness for a week. Pete was using his other team to pull the sprinkler sled used to ice the road so the log sleds would glide easier.

"I'm obliged."

"You take good care of him. I expect you to liniment Viking up and hand walk him."

"Yes sir!"

"And I expect peaches with my flaggin's!"

"Yes sir!"

"And Jamie—"

"Yes sir?"

"Call me Pete. Never been comfortable with sir, even from a sapling like you."

"Yes—okay Pete."

Pete gave a curt nod and went out of the barn to his team. He climbed on the sprinkler wagon, picked up the lines and clucked to the horses. Jamie could hear the horse-shoe calks crunching along the packed snow and ice.

Jamie grabbed a pitchfork and set to work. The pitchfork felt lighter than usual as he flung the soiled straw onto the manure sled. While he worked, he thought about his straw mattress and how good it felt when it was bulging with fresh stuffing. Every week, Jamie would turn the mattress and give it a shake to plump it up. When the straw could no longer be revived, his ma would tear out the end seam on the mattress and they would replace the old straw with fresh. His ma would then re-sew the end. Some of the jacks did this as well, while others seemed content to sleep on a crushed and flattened mattress which could do little to cushion them from the hard, knobby boards of their bunks.

Jamie stared at the pile of soiled straw. This wasn't even fit for horses to sleep on, he thought. Jamie's smile turned to a smirk. If his ma's saw his face, she would know instantly that he was up to mischief. But she wasn't there and the bit of mischief that Jamie was contemplating conformed to the teachings of her Bible. The eye for an eye part, anyway.

———————————

Jamie paused for a moment after entering the men's bunkhouse, trying to adjust his vision in the dark, window-less building. He fumbled through the shadows with only a slit of light spilling from the cracked door and a dim glow from the iron stove to guide him. Where was Flannigan's bunk? Something wet slapped him in the face. He tried to duck away and was nearly strangled by a rope that caught under his chin. Reeling backwards, Jamie crashed into a table, almost upsetting a kerosene lamp. Heart hammering, he felt along the tabletop until his fingers closed around a matchbox. With shaky hands, Jamie removed a match and struck it across the rough tabletop. For a brief moment, the room was illuminated by the tiny flame. Jamie lifted the chimney from the lamp and lit the wick, then shook out the match. He replaced the chimney, lifted the lamp and moved it around surveying the room. The chimney clattered softly in his unsteady hand. He soon found the source of the soggy slap in the face and attempted strangulation. A rope, hung with drying long johns and socks, had been strung from a bunk post to a rafter. One pair of woollies had been knocked askew and seemed to be clinging for life by one arm.

Carrying the lamp, Jamie moved along the bunks looking for a clue indicating which one was Flannigan's. Obviously, they didn't have names on them. Some of the bunks were tidy, blankets folded, extra clothing draped neatly over railings. Others resembled pig sties, blankets rumpled, clothing and meager personal items strewn about. Without fail, each bunk had several wool Hudson Bay blankets. The number of black stripes, or points, indicated the number of beaver pelts required in trade. Jamie remembered Flannigan bragging about his five-point blanket—the only one in camp.

Moving quickly, Jamie worked his way through the thirty bunks. There were a lot of three-point blankets, half-dozen four-pointers, some boasting colorful stripes and some plain. But where was Flannigan's prided five-point? Just as Jamie was about to give up the lamp glow washed over an upper bunk, which was a mess but for a neatly folded blanket. He reached up, lifted a corner, and counted. Five stripes!

Jamie had to set the lamp back on the table to drag the mattress off the top bunk. How could straw be so heavy? With a final heave, it slid off its wooden slats and like a demon seemed to throw itself against Jamie, knocking him off balance so that he sat abruptly on the hard floor. Sweat beaded his brow as he dragged the mattress to the door. He paused, trying to catch his breath, which rasped like a sawyer's blade. Outside he squinted in the daylight. It was well into the morning, though the sun could not penetrate the veil of clouds that hung over camp. It was getting late.

His urgency was turning to panic as he fought to un-seam the mattress. If only he had thought to bring a knife. He must hurry or he would be caught. Ma would come out of the cook shack and see her demented son wrestling with, of all things, a mattress. Or one of the lumberjacks would return to camp to patch up an injury or repair an axe and catch Jamie. What a strange sight indeed! There he would be, boy idiot, chewing on the end of a mattress, the presence of his manure sled heaped with its steaming load adding to the mystery.

Sweat ran in rivulets down Jamie's spine as he bit and chewed at the mattress end. At last, the course thread gave way and he quickly spilled its contents onto the manure sled. Filling the mattress with the soiled straw could not be done with a pitchfork, as Jamie had planned, for the limp material of the mattress would not stand open, but simply collapsed into itself. Jamie would have to stuff the mattress by hand! He contemplated the unsavory task for a moment. If only he had spare gloves or even mittens—a long mitten that would reach to his elbow, like socks that came up to the knees. That was it: a sock! Jamie raced into the bunkhouse, yanked a sock off the clothesline and pulled it over his arm. Sufficiently protected, Jamie returned to the mattress caper. By holding the mattress open with one hand and stuffing with the other, the ticking was soon bulging with fresh manure and soiled straw.

He had not been able to filch a needle and thread from his ma's sewing box, so he had no way to sew the mattress back up. No matter, he would tuck it under.

Jamie ripped off the protective sock/mitten and threw it behind the bunkhouse. He grabbed the open end of the mattress and dragged it, like an overloaded flour sack, back into the bunkhouse. He gasped for air, his chest on the verge of exploding. Many layers below his coat, his drenched long johns clung to his legs, resisting his every step. At last he reached Flannigan's bunk and stopped dead. He craned his neck looking up. What was he thinking? He might as well try to hoist the mattress up a pine tree! It was no use. He had been outwitted by his own plan. Jamie dropped to his knees and with clenched fists pummeled the manure-stuffed mattress. Why was everything so hard? Why wasn't his pa there to help? Pa, so strong—muscles bulging through his long johns—would have hoisted the mattress without breaking a sweat. But the river had taken him, swallowed him like a huge serpent, and all those muscles were no match for the current and the logs that churned in the deadly brew. And Jamie had done nothing, nothing but stand by weak and helpless as a newborn fawn.

A clanging noise bolted Jamie upright. Ma was calling him with the dinner bell to deliver the flaggin's to the men. He stared at the mattress. Sinister, it taunted him. Weakling and dimwit, defeated by a brainless mattress filled with horse dung.

CHAPTER THREE
Flaggin's

The Swede's plump back and thick winter coat gave Jamie the sensation he was riding on a cloud. His ma had wrapped and packed sandwiches and canned fruit into haversacks which were then tied across the Swede's back for carrying to the lumberjacks. Also tucked away were tins of tea for brewing hot drinks in the number-two soup cans that each jack carried hooked onto his suspender button. Jamie rode down the pike-way to his first destination. He tried to savor the ride. He loved the gentle, rhythmic swaying of the big horse's gait. But the fact that Flannigan's mattress still lay in a heap back on the bunkhouse floor could not be shoved into the back of his mind. In the distance, he heard the sharp crack of a tree yielding to the sawyer's blade. Timber! reverberated through the forest, followed by more cracking and snapping as a mighty pine plummeted to earth, its branches and massive trunk ripping away that which stood in its path.

Jamie approached the men working at the fallen tree. The great pine lay paralyzed like a wounded dying giant, while the men moved from limb to limb, snicking them off with their crosscut saws and axes. Jamie halted his horse and watched the scene he had witnessed a hundred times before. After the tree was stripped of limbs and branches, it would be cut to sixteen-foot lengths and branded with the Chicago Lumber Company mark.

"Boy's here with the chuck!" shouted one of the lumberjacks. "Stop your gawking laddie and bring it on."

Jamie nudged the Swede forward into the camp. He slid off the horse and began untying the haversacks.

"Hand me one of those nose sacks boy and make it quick. We got a lot more timber to cut 'fore we get a full skid."

Jamie passed out the food. One of the lumberjacks added wood to a campfire and the men gathered around to eat their lunch.

Jamie had several more stops to make before he would return to camp to resupply. In spite of the many hungry men awaiting their lunch, he hesitated, staring at the landscape. To the north stood the seemingly endless forests of white pine, their majestic boughs reaching for sunlight and enormous trunks standing straight and gallant. Beneath the canopy of these champions, Jamie felt odd stirrings, mystical and heavenly. His pa called it the spirit of the pine. Jamie remembered touching the rough bark of a tree with his pa. "Do you feel its soul?" Pa had asked. Sometimes, if Jamie squeezed his eyes shut and held his breath, he thought he could feel it. Today, the trees seemed to be watching, frozen and quaking, awaiting the rip of the lumberjacks' saws and blows of their axes. Jamie shook his head to rid the thoughts and turned away.

To the south lay a stumpy, wounded landscape, with only a few puny saplings left standing. It looked vulnerable; a weeping pustule that would surely never heal.

"Better get a goin' now, boy, or you'll be havin' the men come lookin' for you," one of the jacks said.

Jamie led the Swede to a stump, sap still oozing. Using the stump as a boost, Jamie mounted. With a cluck and a nudge, they plodded off. It was time to look for Pete Atkins, before the peaches ran out.

He found Pete a mile or so down the pike-way, resting his team. Steam rose through the fibers of the blankets Pete had thrown over the horses.

"You timed it just right," Pete said as he reached up to scratch the nose of one of the horses. "I see the Swede is serving you well."

"Yes sir," Jamie said, dismounting.

Jamie handed him the food. Pete removed a tool from his pocket, a knife of sorts, but with its blades on hinges that folded snugly back into the handle. The knife had more than blades, and Pete extracted a can opener to cut the lid from his peaches. Jamie watched him work the tool and wished he'd had the remarkable invention to work on Flannigan's mattress.

"Want a mouthful, then Jamie?"

"Oh, no sir."

"Pete."

"Pete."

Pete nodded. He closed the opener, pulled out a slender blade and proceeded to spear peach slices and eat them.

"Got to be careful doin' this," Pete said. "Nearly cut off my tongue, once."

"Well, I best be moving on," Jamie said.

"Fore you go, James, I'm wondering if you've been

thinkin' on our talk this morning."

Uneasiness washed over Jamie. He had nearly forgotten his tomfoolery with the mattress.

"I...ah...well," Jamie muttered.

"I started thinkin'," Pete said, "maybe I shouldn't be putting ideas into a boy's head. You pull somethin' on Flannigan, and he may rip you to pieces and feed you to the wolves."

Jamie stood in horror; his thoughts racing in a jumbled frenzy.

"You'll have your chance, James, in a few years. Maybe won't be Flannigan, but you'll get some meat on you and the jacks will think twice before they have fun at your expense."

"But...I"

"Best advice is to bide your time, James, and stay out of the way best you can."

The can of peaches gone, Pete unfolded the towel that held his sandwiches. He took a huge bite, chewing thoughtfully.

"Not that I wouldn't mind seein' old Flannigan get his comeuppance," Pete said. "Any man picks on a boy is a coward." Pete stopped chewing for a moment. "Course, Larry picks on everybody, 'cept his wife. Acts like a whipped puppy around her. He took me home with him last Christmas. Lord, what a wild bunch his children are. His wife, Meghan, looks delicate as a fawn, but inside lives a wildcat. I'd rather bed down with a den of wolves than spend a night in that house again."

Jamie knew what living in a wilderness cabin was like. A long winter could give anybody a case of the shacknasties. He remembered when his pa first started working for the logging company. He had built a small cabin outside the town of Seney to house Jamie and Ma, then commenced his logging job with the Chicago Lumber Company. Days stretched into weeks between visits from his pa, and his ma grew restless and irritable. Often, she paced the tiny cabin, staring for hours out its only window. Jamie's pa came home when he could. Sometimes he would snowshoe for hours or hitch a ride, just to spend a few hours on a Sunday with his wife and son. But he was more like a visitor than a pa, sometimes almost a stranger. Then he would be gone and the gray, bleak days of the Michigan winter would trudge on endlessly.

Pete chewed thoughtfully, swallowing with effort. "Nope, Flannigan's missus can't hold a candle to your ma. Trouble with the Irish is they live like there was no tomorrow. I ask you Jamie boy, how can a man go to town on a Saturday night and spend his hard-earned wages on whiskey, then brawl and fight 'til he's got to be brought home draped over his horse like a deer carcass? Same man goes to church the next day, pious as a preacher. Nope, the Irish take too much to their liquor and fists, you ask me."

Liquor: the root of all evil, Ma always said. Jamie thought back again of the little wilderness cabin. It seemed so long ago, though actually less than a year. Ma and Pa had quarreled, their voices rising, louder and louder. Jamie had hidden in the wood shack, afraid to breathe, afraid to move. She had accused his pa of imbibing in whiskey. It was a sin to partake of alcohol, she had shouted, and he would surely be sentenced to eternal damnation for his heathen ways. Pa had stomped out, returning to camp early.

The Home Wind

The weeks had passed with no word from him. Ma said little during those weeks, her face pinched and worried. Finally, one day she told Jamie to pack his belongings. When he had asked where they were going, she said that his pa was a stubborn ox, but it was her duty as a Christian woman to care for him. And it was not too late for his salvation she had added with resolve.

Pete finished off the last bite of sandwich and handed the towel it had been wrapped in back to Jamie.

"And the food that little Meghan Flannigan serves I wouldn't feed to a cur. Not like your ma, James, no indeed. Now, the Widow Kangas knows how to fuel a man. I guess we better both be getting on with our work. No good idling away the day," Pete said.

Jamie nodded and moved over to the Swede. Pete gave him a boost up. It felt good to have the horse's warmth back.

"No sir, your ma would skin me if she knew I was keeping you from your chores."

It was true, Jamie was running dangerously behind. There would never be time to work his schooling into the day. Perhaps his ma would forget to ask about it. Not likely. Jamie urged the Swede into a trot. The big horse moved with a steady smooth gait so, in spite of having no saddle, Jamie was able to stay on with only occasionally grabbing a fistful of the coarse mane.

A horse sure beat walking. If a body had to walk in the winter, snowshoes made the going possible, but it was still mighty hard work. Jamie and his ma had walked for miles on their snowshoes, pulling the sled bundled with their belongings and food. The wind had been bitter and Jamie's hands and feet had gone numb. They had arrived at his pa's logging camp at dusk, exhausted and nearly frozen. The sound of the dinner bell had helped guide them into camp. Jamie and his Ma had staggered up to the cook shack and removed their snowshoes.

"Wait here, son," she had said to Jamie.

"But, I'm so cold." Jamie said, his teeth chattering.

"I won't be a minute."

Jamie had watched her pause at the door. She seemed to pull herself up. She smoothed her hair back under her hat and brushed the snow from her clothing, then yanked open the door and marched in. Jamie could only imagine the reaction of the lumberjacks when she confronted his pa. It was rare that an unescorted woman entered a lumber camp and unimaginable that a wife would come to fetch her man. Soon they had emerged and Pa took her arm and led her to large, crude log building: the men's bunkhouse. His ma had turned around and shouted for Jamie to follow.

And now Jamie was chore boy at the camp, which wasn't so bad when he got to ride the Swede. The horse stepped out smartly, arching his neck, extending his gait. Jamie gave him a nudge and the horse broke into a canter. The mighty hooves clopped along, the horseshoe calks sending ice chips flying in all directions. Jamie's eyes stung with tears and his cheeks burned from the cold, but he didn't care. This was heaven, galloping now, along the icy road. Jamie hunched over the Swede's neck feeling the mane brush his face. He could hear the steady, rhythmic roll of the horse's nostrils expelling the frigid air. Jamie grinned with joy and peered out of squinting, blurred eyes. He was hypnotized by the sound of hoof beats and haversacks flapping against the horse.

"Away we go, away we go!" he sang under his breath.

Jamie felt the Swede hesitate, his stride collecting, slowing. Jamie wondered why they were slowing as he tried to open his stinging eyes to focus.

Something loomed ahead, hazy and serpentine. A tree! Before Jamie could haul back on the reins to slow the Swede, the horse gathered himself and launched into the air with spectacular ease. Jamie felt the mane slip from his grasp as he catapulted off the horse and landed with a soft thud in a deep snowdrift. He lay still for a moment, winded and disoriented. He listened to a diminishing noise—a muffled cadence of hoof beats. When he finally sat up, Jamie realized it was the sound of the Swede. Headed back to camp, Jamie guessed, with the flaggin's!

Jamie stood and brushed himself off. He neck was stiff and he could only turn his head one direction. Both elbows tingled, and snow that had somehow found its way inside his pants was beginning to melt.

"If I make it back without freezing, won't matter," Jamie mumbled as he set out on foot. "They'll skin me and roast me alive sure as I'm standing here. Then Larry Flannigan can take my carcass and cut it up for the wolves."

Jamie considered not going back. Maybe he could make it to the ill-reputed town of Seney and get a job in a saloon. He had heard there were dozens of them. No, that would all but kill his ma. Maybe he could go back to their old cabin and become a recluse. Woodsmen did it; he'd heard stories.

Some said these men had a disease called solitude. They made a little money for liquor and bacon by trapping animals and selling the pelts. They didn't have to bathe, ever. Didn't have to use a fork or wipe their mouth or study the Bible or sweep the floor. Nobody told them what to do. Anybody came around who wasn't welcome the woodsman pulled out his gun and ran him off, simple as that.

But was the cabin still there? And how would he get there without snowshoes or food?

Jamie shook his head gloomily. No, he would have to go back and face his ma and the men who never got their lunch. They might even try to thrash him. What chance would he have against a bunch of men who could wrestle an ox to the ground with one arm?

Besides, what would Ma do without him? Who would help her if he were gone? The fact that they had let a woman, the wife of a lumberman at that, become camp cook was unusual enough.

Jamie had to admire his ma's spunk when she had barged in on Pa's lumber camp. Jamie had obediently followed them into the men's bunkhouse on that day of reckoning. Pa had asked her whatever had possessed her to come. Why, she and the boy could have frozen to death, Pa had said. But his scolding had a softness. Ma had told him that either she'd stay here and do whatever was needin' to be done or she and Jamie would be taking a train back east to live with her sister. She made it clear that under no circumstances would she go back to that miserable little cabin.

Jamie didn't much relish the thought of returning to that cabin then or now, even if he was provisioned for the journey. Its memory held a lot more grief than joy. He stared down at the Swede's hoof prints, which likely led back to the camp. A horse would take the shortest way back to the stable, homing in on a warm stall and a manger of hay. Jamie came upon the haversacks, which had fallen from the horse, their contents flung about and half-buried in the snow. Jamie gathered what he could find and stuffed it into the sacks. As he dragged them along, they floundered in the snow making it as difficult to haul them as the mattress. The mattress! He had nearly forgotten. Why did he ever try to pull that prank? He was a fool! Jamie thrust himself against the loaded sacks, trudging along as best he could. Perhaps he could pull the manure mattress out into the woods and hide it then give Flannigan his own mattress. Of course, he would never be able to get it back onto the top bunk and how would he explain the disappearance of his own mattress to his ma?

Jamie felt his own stomach rumble and thought of the lumberjacks growing angry with hunger. He stopped a minute and pulled a sandwich out of a sack, taking a huge bite. It was good, being able to get his fill of food. Being the son of the camp cook had its advantages. There had been days back in the cabin when Jamie's belly had growled and rumbled because provisions often ran low between visits from Pa. At the logging camp, food was plentiful and days were not nearly so lonely. Jamie guessed that he was lucky for that. It was a stroke of luck, if not an act of God, what the foreman Tom Haskins had said about Jamie's ma walking into camp that day.

Their timing had been good because the camp cook had gone to town with a pocketful of company greenbacks to get supplies and had vanished. Not only had the scallywag stolen company money, which would land him in the poky when they caught up to him, but he left the lumberjacks in a lurch. Tom Haskins had sent a man to Seney to seek a replacement but the decadent town had likely swallowed him as well, for his return was well past due. The men grew surly and restless, eating cold meals out of tin cans and suffering from coffee that could tan a hide. Haskins was unable to control the men's brawling and there had been rumblings of a mutiny. In spite of her exhaustion, Jamie's ma had stepped in that very night and made biscuits, deer-meat stew, and a dried-apple cobbler. She was offered the position of camp cook and, in spite of her husband's protests, accepted the offer.

Jamie enjoyed having a full belly. Running away was out of the question. He paused a minute, stamping his feet and clapping his arms around his torso to warm himself. Of course, nobody needed know that he and the Swede had been larking. Maybe it had been an accident; the Swede had spooked or stumbled. Maybe his ma would be terribly worried, the men's midday hunger secondary to her boy's well-being. But how would he deal with the mattress?

Jamie stopped again and mulled this over. Of course, nobody had seen him. Like Pete said, he owed Flannigan one. Probably a lot of the jacks owed Flannigan one. Just in case though, Jamie had to come up with a plan. When he started walking again, he practiced limping. He was getting close to camp now and believed he had mastered a very convincing limp. The weight of the sacks, which he was still dragging, surely added to the spectacle. Once again, things were looking up. The chore boy had taken a spill, that's all. He would stoically limp into camp, a wretched exhibit for all to see. Perhaps Ma would try to sooth him and comfort him with a cookie or other sweet. Mattress? Jamie would know nothing of a mattress. The idea of thrashing a crippled boy was unimaginable even to the most lawless lumberjack.

"Hey, pick on somebody your own size," the jacks would taunt Flannigan. "What kind of man are you, tormenting that poor crippled boy!"

Jamie fought away his smirk. Ma would know that face so he must control it. She would be the true test, Ma, thought Jamie as he limped into the clearing of the camp.

CHAPTER FOUR
Battles

Pete arrived for supper with a shiner of a black eye. Larry Flannigan was not in much better shape, his lip cracked and swollen and the remnants of dried blood crusting his beard. Obeying the rule of mealtime silence, there was no discussion of what had obviously been a fistfight. Jamie's ma clucked her tongue in disapproval at the two men who hunched miserably over their plates. They had seated themselves at opposite ends of the table, but managed to cast hateful glances at one another throughout the meal. Flannigan appeared to have trouble eating his stew, the swollen lip interfering. The puffiness around Pctc's eye progressed quickly until he was peering through a ghastly, purple slit.

Jamie paused at Pete's side, slowly pouring coffee into his cup.

"It was a fair plan Jamie boy," Pete whispered, "but you might have thought it through better."

It was the mattress, thought Jamie! Pete had taken the blame for the botched scheme.

Jamie heard the man next to Pete snicker. He looked up to see that the Widow Kangas had moved away into the kitchen. "It were a fine one, lad. Too bad Pete here took the brunt. Still, it were worth it, eh Pete?"

The Home Wind

Pete grunted and touched his fingers to his eye. "Not you who took a sucker punch, Roy."

"Ah, that'll heal. Now Flannigan, he's got a missing tooth, and I don't think the tooth fairy will be bringin' 'em a new un."

The foreman, Tom Haskins, stood for a moment and hissed, "You men hush, or none of us will get pie."

Jamie's ma entered the room carrying a pie in each hand.

"James," she snapped.

Jamie slammed down the coffee pot. He rushed to meet her and took the pies. He avoided looking up, but could feel her eyes boring into him. She knew, she knew! Maybe not exactly what, but she was onto something. Jamie hurried to deliver the pies and scurried back into the kitchen. His ma stood over the stove, starting to heat the dishwater.

"Perhaps you can share your medicinal secrets with Mr. Atkins and Mr. Flannigan who seem to have come to blows," she said.

"Medicinal secrets?" Jamie said.

"Why yes, son. Never have I seen so miraculous a recovery," she said, turning from the stove. She placed her hands on her hips and faced her son, her look drilling into him like a hot poker.

"Wha . . . what do you mean?" Jamie said.

"Why your ankle, James, it seems to have healed completely."

Jamie had forgotten to limp! He made a pathetic attempt to resume his staged injury. "I have to go get the coffee pot," he said, limping with renewed vigor.

"Oh James?"

"Yes 'um?"

"I thought it was your left ankle, dear. Now you seem to be lame on the right. Please make up your mind."

Jamie's cheeks burned. He was greeted with a roar of laughter from the lumberjacks who had overheard the admonishment. All pretense of a sprained ankle gone, Jamie fled the mess hall and ran out into the cold, dark night. He shivered in the chill. His Mackinaw was inside hanging on its peg.

A full moon slid from behind a cloud, illuminating the camp. Snowflakes drifted down, falling light as feathers to the ground. He remembered when he used to catch them on his tongue. He remembered when he played in the snow, his fort constructed to withstand the onslaughts of his cousins' snowballs. It seemed so long ago when he and Ma visited with his aunt and uncle in their big house out East. That was before Pa had taken them into the wilderness.

Lost in his thoughts, Jamie found himself shivering outside the stable. He entered, thankful for the warmth. The stable was nearly pitch dark. A horse nickered, hoping for an extra ration of oats. Jamie remembered that there was a lantern in the smithy's shed off the stable. He decided to feel his way there and retrieve it. He could check on the Swede and make sure he was warm and dry after his unscheduled gallop back to camp. Jamie felt his way through the dark, with only dim pinpricks of moonlight seeping through cracks in the wall chinking. The horses and stalls, mere silhouettes, blended into shadowy darkness.

Jamie finally reached the smithy's shed and fumbled along a workbench until he found the lantern. He was searching his pockets for a match when he heard a noise. It wasn't the sound of a horse shifting around in its stall, nor was it the scurrying noise made by the ever-present vermin. It was a human sound—muffled, maybe a cough. Jamie fingered a match, finally located in the depths of his pocket. All of the men were still at supper. No one should be in the stable.

Silently, Jamie pulled the match from his trousers. He willed his jagged breathing to slow, certain that whoever, whatever was lurking in the stable would hear his rasping breaths.

Then he heard it again. Definitely a cough. Not the kind one used to clear his throat but a croupy noise.

"Who . . . who's there?" Jamie said, his voice barely above a whisper. More coughing—stronger.

It was coming from a corner of the barn. Jamie struck the match and lit the lantern. "Who's there!" he said with more conviction.

Jamie took the lantern and slowly moved toward the coughing. He inched his way along the wall, forcing his leaden legs into action.

"Now come out! Come out this instant or I'll go get the men." Jamie hung the lantern on a peg and balled his fists, readying for the unknown.

Something darted from the corner and barreled toward Jamie. He felt the wind forced from his chest as he hit the ground. They thrashed around, grunting, banging into the log walls and rolling under a stall divider into a horse's hooves. Jamie tried to pummel the intruder with his fists, but the ungainly embrace restricted his swing and his blows fell harmless. At last Jamie managed to maneuver himself topside and he stretched his opponent's arms out, pinning them to the cold dirt floor.

He stared into the face of his defeated foe, feeling the chest rapidly rise and fall beneath him. Tangled hair, long and dark, splayed across the dirt. Hair like a girl's, but it was the face of a boy and it wore trousers. The boy coughed.

"Get off me you bastard," he wheezed.

"Hey, watch - your - tongue, or - I'll - cut - it - out," Jamie said through gasps of air. The boy coughed again, his feverish eyes glistening in the lantern glow. Jamie loosened his grip.

"Promise not to run?" Jamie said. The boy nodded.

Jamie climbed off and the boy sat up.

He was certainly odd. His clothing hung in tatters and rags bound his feet.

"Who are you? What's your name and whatta ya doing here?" Jamie said.

"I am Gray Feather," the boy said. "I am Ojibwa."

An Indian! Jamie had just licked an Indian! Jamie waited but Gray Feather was coughing, unable to talk, then his head lolled to the side and his body went limp. It took a minute for Jamie to realize that the Indian he had bravely defeated was sick and had fainted. Some victory, he thought, besting a sick Indian boy.

Jamie heard the sounds of the jacks outside. They were leaving the mess hall and heading to their bunks. What should he do? Get one of the men, get his ma or just leave the boy—this Gray Feather—and hope that he'd be gone

The Home Wind

in the morning? Jamie peered down at his new charge and listened to his rattled breathing. How did this bedraggled creature come to the logging camp? The nearest Indian reservation was a great distance away.

Jamie sighed. He definitely couldn't get the men. He had heard their talk of Indians, full of scorn and loathing. One of the jacks told a story of an Indian lumberjack who fell into the river. The other men were resting on the bank but nobody saw fit to give him a hand out of the water. Turned out he couldn't swim and drowned. Since he was a heathen he was never even dragged out of the river for a Christian burial. Jamie shuddered. Nobody deserved that treatment.

Gray Feather moaned and muttered some nonsense that Jamie didn't understand. Ma. Jamie rose and hurried to the cook shack.

CHAPTER FIVE
Gray Feather

"Looks like a half breed to me," said Tom Haskins, glaring at Gray Feather who rested on Jamie's bunk.

"Where'd you come from, boy?" Haskins demanded, bending over and shouting into the sick boy's face.

"His name's Gray Feather. Says he's Ojibwa," Jamie said.

Gray Feather lay silent on the bunk, his face flushed with fever, breathing with difficulty. There was strength, though, in his defiant gaze.

Haskins waved Jamie off. "Should have a white name. You know, a Christian name. What's your white name, boy? Joseph, Billy? I reckon he's a Chippewa—'jibway— same thing. That's mostly what's around here, those that are left."

"Those that haven't been robbed of their land."

Jamie and Tom Haskins turned around to see Pete standing in the doorway.

"This territory legally belongs to the Chicago Lumber Company," Haskins said.

"Indians were swindled," Pete said. "You and I both know it."

"You best be remembering where your pay comes from this spring, Pete, or maybe you want to quit being a jack," Haskins snapped.

"What is the meaning of this?"

The Home Wind

Everyone turned to see Jamie's ma standing in the cook shack doorway.

"I will not have you men talking politics around this sick child nor around my son, for that matter."

"Yes, Ma'am," Haskins said, "but you see, we can't be keeping this Indian boy here. If he's got no ma or pa, he's got to be turned over to the Bureau."

"You'll not be turning him over to anybody. Least not 'til he's well. Now out!"

Pete and Tom scrambled out the door, trying to squeeze through at the same time, their broad shoulders jamming in the door frame.

"Get out of my way you blasted fool," said Tom, shoving Pete aside.

It was Sunday morning, the only day of rest allowed at the lumber camp. Rest for the men, but not for the cook, because the men still had to eat. Jamie and his ma had foregone their morning worship to tend to Gray Feather. Ma had prepared an herbal steam to ease the sick boy's labored breathing. He had not resisted her special brew of honeyed tea to sooth his cough.

"He's nearly starved and frozen. Look at his feet, wrapped in tattered rags. Lord have mercy! I can't get a word out of him," she said. "Turn this wretched child over to the Bureau of Indian Affairs? Indeed. Why they'll stick him in some disease-infested orphanage to die."

She held a spoonful of soup to Gray Feather's lips. He shifted himself, sitting upright, and took the spoon.

"I am not a babe," he said.

"It would be wise to hold your sass," Jamie whispered.

40

Gray Feather ignored Jamie and abandoning his spoon, lifted the soup bowl to his lips and slurped hungrily.

"It might also be wise to use eating utensils," Jamie added.

Ma was surprisingly tolerant of the Indian boy's inexcusable behavior—an indulgence Jamie had never himself enjoyed.

"You keep an eye on him James, while I go to the meat shed," Ma said. She put on her overcoat and stepped out of the cook shack.

Jamie and Gray Feather sat for a moment in silence, the Indian boy staring at the ceiling. "Your mother is good," Gray Feather said.

Jamie nodded.

"Stern like the nuns but not cruel like the white men."

"Nuns?" Jamie said.

"I spent some time with the Sisters before they closed the school."

"School? You went to school?" Jamie asked.

Gray Feather nodded and looked into his empty soup bowl.

"I have learned to read and write and have read much of the Bible. We were never to speak Chippewa or tell stories of our ancestors or use Ojibwa names. I have a white name, Charlie, as the man said. Sister Harriet said that to use an un-Christian name was the sign of a heathen."

Jamie had heard of heathens: godless people who danced naked around fires, cast evil spells on their enemies, and made blood sacrifices to the devil. Jamie shifted uncomfortably.

The Home Wind

"Where are your mother and father?" he asked.

Gray Feather turned his gaze from the ceiling to Jamie. His unwavering look penetrated like that of a wolf.

"My mother is dead. I am searching for my father."

"Who is your father? Is he on a reservation?"

"No. He is not Ojibwa. He is white."

Then Gray Feather—Charlie—was a half-breed as Haskins said.

The two boys were again silent. Gray Feather turned his attention back to the ceiling, staring. His chest rose and fell in an even rhythm, no longer ragged. His eyelids fluttered closed.

No! Jamie thought, he can't be asleep. There were so many more questions. What was it like, being an Indian? Was it true that their ancestors lived in wigwams and paddled birch bark canoes and hunted with bows and arrows? Jamie had read about them in a book that his cousin had once lent him. It was so exciting, so adventurous! And what about his father? How would he ever find him?

All this remained a mystery locked inside the restless, sleeping Indian boy. He did not look like a Charlie at all. Such a name conjured up images of a clownish, happy fellow, not the solemn, haunted boy who now slept fitfully on Jamie's bunk. Jamie vowed to always call him by his Ojibwa name: Gray Feather.

———————

After two weeks of herbal teas, pungent soups, and rest Gray Feather grew strong and willful. Jamie's ma had kept the boy warm and quiet until she could no longer control his restlessness. Soon Gray Feather was following Jamie around, helping with chores. The teamsters now had two chore boys to order about and Jamie was grateful.

But that was not the only benefit. Jamie never tired of hearing Gray Feather's stories. Jamie went through the motions of his daily chores, eager for the day's end when they would sit cross-legged on Gray Feather's sleeping pallet in the stable. There they would exchange a bit of food saved back from supper along with stories.

"The white man does not want us to tell our stories," Gray Feather said one night. "You must not tell any of the men in this camp, or even your mother."

"Why not?" Jamie said.

"They must not know that I have been given these stories to remember; to pass on when the time comes. This is not something the white man wants. If we forget, it will be as though it never happened."

"But you have told me."

Gray Feather smiled. "I know I can trust you. You do not hold the hatred for me like the others. You have proven that in many ways. You gave me your bed when I was sick."

"But it was Ma who nursed you." Jamie said. "Don't you trust her?"

Gray Feather shook his head. "Not completely, though I will always be grateful to her."

"But I don't understand," Jamie said, frustrated. "Who doesn't want the stories to pass on? Ma wouldn't try to stop you."

"It is difficult to explain. But you must remember who owns this camp—who these people work for. There are the people who rule: the lumber companies, the Washington chiefs— congressmen."

The Home Wind

Jamie shook his head, confused. "I remember when I was real little, Grandpappy Eero— that was Grandpappy's first name, Eero—anyway, Grandpappy Eero came to visit us in Michigan. He told stories about Finland where he and Grandma were born. Later, he and Grandma moved to Canada. That's where my pa was born, in Canada. He met Ma there. Ma says she was just a girl working in a dry goods store when this pale-haired, blue-eyed lumberjack stopped in for supplies. Sweet- talked her something fierce, Ma said. Before she knew it, she married up with him and they worked their way into Michigan, looking for work. Somewhere along the line, I was born. Anyway, I remember Grandpappy Eero always said it was important to pass stories about the family, keep them alive, in a way. Why isn't it the same for the Indians?"

Gray Feather did not answer right away. "Your grandfather and grandmother, were they forced from their land?"

Jamie pondered this question for a moment. "No. I don't think so, not really forced. But they were very poor and Grandpappy said they went to Canada because there was opportunity and maybe a little adventure. I remember him saying, ya, yer grandma don't tink much of da adventure, dat's fer sure. He whispered as if Grandma would overhear him, even though she was dead and buried."

Gray Feather nodded and stared off into the darkness of the stable.

"My people were always part of this land," he said, stretching his arms outward. "The Algonquin were here in ancient times. From those people came the Ojibwa or Chippewa as we are called. In times past, we joined with the

Ottawa and Pottawatomi tribes and our three tribes were called the Council of Three Fires. The Ojibwa are the keepers of faith, the Ottawa are the keepers of trade, and the Potawatomi are the keepers of the fire. The name Ojibwa refers to the gathered seam of the moccasin."

"You were named after a… a moccasin?" Jamie said.

Gray Feather smiled and shrugged his shoulders. "Not exactly."

It was the first time Jamie had seen Gray Feather smile.

"Sometimes something that appears small and unimportant is really much more than it seems."

Jamie thought on that for a while. Small and unimportant, like him.

"Take a single grain of rice: *mah-no-mo-nee* it is called in Ojibwa. Alone it is not enough to feed even the tiniest bird, but if it is allowed to grow it will sprout many grains of rice, perhaps a handful, enough to feed that bird. If the handful of rice is not eaten and ripens and falls into the water, it will grow into many more plants with enough rice to feed a man."

Gray Feather took a bite from a cookie that Jamie had pinched from his mother's larder.

The Indian boy chewed thoughtfully. "My mother never made these," he said holding up the remains of his cookie. "And there was nothing like this at the school. Tell your mother than I would like these all the time. I will thank her tomorrow for this one."

Jamie shifted uncomfortably on the pallet. "Well, I'm sure that she would be happy that you like her cookies, it's just that she doesn't exactly know that you have that cookie."

The Home Wind

Gray Feather paused a moment, contemplating the last bit of cookie, then popped it in his mouth. "I do not understand. What cookie does she think I have? Aren't they all the same?"

Jamie squirmed and uncrossed his legs, trying to decide how to explain. "You see, ah, well, I kind of took it without her knowing . . . exactly."

Gray Feather snapped his head around and looked at Jamie. "Then it was stolen? But one must never steal from his own clan." He wiped a few crumbs from his mouth and looked at them. "And it is gone. I cannot give it back."

"Oh, it's not really stolen. More like snitched. It's okay to snitch food now and then. Ma will slap my hand away if she catches me with my fingers in the dough, but she isn't really angry. I think she is actually pleased."

"She is pleased that you steal?" Gray Feather said. "The nuns told us it was a sin to steal."

Jamie sighed. "I can't explain it any better. There are some things that you are expected to steal." He thought a moment. "Imagine that we are sitting around a fire."

Gray Feather nodded.

"We both sit close to the fire and are nice and warm. But the wind is to my back and in your face and all the smoke is going toward you. I get up to, ah, maybe to get another cookie…"

"A stolen cookie," Gray Feather said, nodding.

Jamie pounded his fist on his legs. "No! It's not a stolen cookie, it's—well anyway, I get up and leave and even though you know I'm coming back, you move to the spot where the smoke is not going into your face, because it is a better spot and steal it from me."

"Is it summer or winter?" Gray Feather asked.

Jamie sighed. "What difference does that make?"

"If it was summer, then I would move so that you could sit in the smoke as an offering of my friendship."

"Giving someone the smoky spot is an offering of friendship?" Jamie said, exasperated.

Gray Feather nodded. "Yes, because the smoke keeps the bites of insects away in the summer." He smiled and looked proudly at Jamie. "Yes, you are my friend and I would definitely give you the smoky spot in the summer. In the winter, I would let you inside my cabin. I would not make you sit outside in the snow. Just as you let me sleep in your bed when I was sick and have given me a warm place in the barn with the horses."

Jamie felt a wave of guilt. He and his ma had wanted Gray Feather to sleep in the cook shack with them, but Tom Haskins would not have that half breed bunking with the Widow Kangas. The men's bunk house was out of the question. The Indian boy would be tormented by the lumberjacks. So the barn it was, with only a straw pallet and blankets for warmth and a single lantern for light. Yet, Gray Feather seemed content and Ma and Jamie made certain that he had plenty to eat. Mother said she would fatten him up. Gray Feather was thirteen—a year older than Jamie, but not even an inch taller and much thinner. Ma speculated his growth was stunted by years of poor nourishment.

"And your mother has given me these fine boots," Gray Feather said, pointing toward his feet. "I do not mind the rags in the toes, though I find it a strange custom."

The Home Wind

Jamie shook his head. It was hopeless, explaining things to an Indian. The rags in the toes were to make the too-large boots fit. It wasn't that Gray Feather was stupid. In fact he was very clever at times. It was just that he thought about things differently. Who sat around thinking about a grain of rice? Still, it was comforting, in a way, the idea of something small becoming big and important. Jamie Kangas: a mere grain of rice was something important waiting to happen. He laughed to himself. Gray Feather looked at him.

"What is funny?"

Jamie shook his head. "You wouldn't understand."

"Like the cookie?" Gray Feather asked.

"Forget the cookie, will you?" said Jamie.

"How can I forget? Now that I have had one, I will think of nothing else."

"I will make sure you get lots of cookies."

"You will steal more for me?"

Jamie had to laugh. Gray Feather smiled and laughed too. It felt good, to laugh and not be laughed at. Both boys stood and Gray Feather picked up the lantern.

"Yes. I will steal more for you. I'm sure Ma won't mind. I think she likes you. Watch out, though, she is talking of cutting off your hair."

Gray Feather's lifted his hand to his shoulder-length hair and frowned.

Gray Feather and Jamie walked to the stable door. They paused and looked into the star-studded sky.

"The moon is full," Gray Feather said. "It reminds me of a story about the Thunderbird stealing the moon from the sky, thinking it was the face of the enemy."

"Oh, tell me the story, please!" Jamie said.

Gray Feather shook his head. "Some other time, my friend. I will do it for a cookie."

Both boys laughed, and Jamie hurried through the bitter air to the warmth of his bed.

CHAPTER SIX
Stories

Delivering the flaggin's did not take nearly so long with Gray Feather helping. They divided the task, riding in different sectors to cover more ground, Jamie on the Swede and Gray Feather astride a bay gelding named Max. Jamie had hoped to gain some free time from the arrangement, but any thought of that quickly vanished when his mother filled the afternoon with an extra hour of studies.

"Charlie has twenty matchsticks. He gives seven to you, James, and then takes four more. How many matchsticks does he have?"

"Charlie, I want you to tell me what Jesus said to God when…"

"James, you go to the store with a dollar to purchase some sugar that is eight cents a pound. How many pounds can you buy with your dollar?"

It was a dreary prospect. Jamie could see no need to know how many matchsticks were in a box. A big bunch meant he had enough, a few meant he was running low and should stock up. Let the storekeeper figure out how much change he had coming when he bought sugar. That was his job, wasn't it?

However, Jamie and Gray Feather stole a few minutes from this drudgery lingering at a special meeting place.

The Home Wind

"I have extra grub," Jamie said, halting his horse next to Gray Feather's." One of the jacks broke a stem and they had to cart him off to the hospital. They left without their food. It was Ollie Anderson. They say it looks bad." Jamie shook his head.

"A stem?" Gray Feather said.

Jamie nodded. "Yeah, his leg—real bad."

Jamie and Gray Feather had ridden to their rendezvous point at a small lake that was frozen solid and blanketed with snow. The absence of trees made it easy to spot.

"How did he do this...break a stem?" Gray Feather said.

"He was skyhooking. You know, he was on top of the logs while they were stacking them on the sled. A blue butt got hoisted up—that's a log with one end much bigger than the other— and when he tried to saginaw her into place, it shifted on him, sent the whole pile off kilter. I guess Ollie jumped clear, but bent his leg when he landed wrong. If he hadn't jumped, though, they would have been callin' the sky pilot for sure—that's a priest."

Gray Feather stared at Jamie for a moment. "What is this language you are speaking," he asked.

"I dunno. Jack talk, I guess."

Gray Feather dismounted. Jamie hopped off his horse and dug a bundle out of the haversack while Gray Feather tied the horses to a tree. The two boys spread a blanket and sat, legs crossed. They unwrapped their lunch and began eating.

"I'm getting tired of deer meat," Jamie said. "There is not much else in the meat shed, Ma says. Only some sowbelly and the deer. Ma says you can tell spring is comin' because her larder is getting lean and the chickens are dwindling. Guess there's no one to make the trip this month to Seney for supplies. Haskins says he can't spare those that he's known long enough to trust and he doesn't want to risk sending a new man who'd likely as not skip off with the greenbacks."

Gray Feather nodded. "Yes, I have noticed that there are many thieves in the forest. The lumberjack, he will steal your boots. This is not so bad, because you can steal them back. But the lumber company, they steal your land when you are too weak to stop them. The worst thief—the worst thief of all is the one who steals the spirit from another."

"But how can someone steal a spirit? I mean I have heard of breaking a spirit, but stealing?"

Gray Feather sat in silence, leaving Jamie's questions unanswered.

"The sun is getting higher," Gray Feather said, "the days longer. Soon I will be able to continue the search for my father."

"But I don't want you to go!" Jamie said. "Why can't you stay here—stay with the lumber camp—at least until the spring drive. You will, won't you?"

Gray Feather shrugged and looked at the frozen lake.

"What is the name of this lake?" Gray Feather asked.

"I dunno.. It's just some lake. Probably hasn't got a name."

"Then you and I should name it."

"Sure, but what?" Jamie said.

Both studied the lake for a moment, thoughtfully chewing their food.

"I can't think of anything," Jamie said.

The Home Wind

"Nor I. This is the place we come to tell stories."

"Story Lake!" they said in unison then laughed. They were beginning to think alike.

"The name was there, waiting to come out," Gray Feather said.

"I dunno. I was named after someone in the Bible—well, James, but everyone calls me Jamie. Except sometimes Ma calls me James Matthew when she's mad at me."

Jamie looked at Gray Feather. "What about your name? Where did it come from?"

"It is because I am not pure," Gray Feather said.

Jamie gave his friend a strange look. "Pure?"

"My mother said I reminded her of the evening as it turns into darkness and the color disappears. Not bright or dark but gray like the twilight. In between. Mixed. And when I was a babe, she said I was quiet as a feather."

Jamie thought about this for a moment. He envied his friend for having a name that told who he was, like the lake. Jamie smiled. He remembered Gray Feather's promise.

"You must tell the story about the Thunderbird. You promised weeks ago!" Jamie said.

"I did promise, but you were to steal more cookies." Gray Feather looked expectantly at Jamie.

Jamie frowned. "Ma says sugar is low. She must save what there is for the pies and for the men's coffee."

Gray Feather sighed. "No matter. I will tell the story."

The boys sat on their blanket and stared at the frozen lake. A raven swooped from a tree, its raucous cawing piercing the silence.

Gray Feather stood, spreading his arms like wings. "Ojibwa legend tells of the Thunderbird, Kenu, the great winged monster who incites destructive winds with its huge wings and sends torrents of water to earth," Gray Feather said, the pitch of his voice rising.

A thunderstorm, thought Jamie.

"With insatiable fury, the Thunderbird uproots trees and flashes fire from its eyes, striking tall pines that explode and burn." Gray Feather was shouting, his arms imitating the great wings of the thunderbird.

"Lightning!" Jamie cried.

Gray Feather held up his hand for silence. He lowered his arms. His voice softened. "Legend says that the Thunderbird passed over a lake one day—a lake very much like this one—only it was summer and the winds were sleeping, letting the water rest in a smooth, clear pool, like a mirror." Gray Feather flattened his hand, palm down, and made a motion as if smoothing the ripples from the water.

Jamie's mind wandered. He thought of summertime—the warmth of the sun, the buzzing insects and fish jumping in the rivers. His father had promised to teach him to fish. Someday.

"The Thunderbird passed over the lake and saw its reflection in the placid water. It mistook its reflection for the face of its enemy and, conjuring its greatest power, reached heavenward and pulled the moon from the sky and thrust it toward the offending image." Gray Feather reached skyward and grasped an imaginary moon.

"Wow," Jamie said.

Gray Feather thrust the imaginary moon toward the frozen lake. "The moon plunged into the lake with a great eruption," Gray Feather boomed, "churning the waters into a frothing mass that dispelled the Thunderbird's reflection." Gray Feather pinwheeled his arms like the demented bird he spoke of. "Satisfied it had conquered its foe, the Thunderbird flapped its powerful wings and flew off. But when the moon returned to the sky it left its image behind, which can be seen in the still waters of every lake during a night of the shining moon." Gray Feather dropped his arms to his side then sat back on the blanket.

"Left its image behind," Jamie said. "Sometimes that never goes away—like a scar."

Gray Feather looked with curiosity at Jamie. "That is true. There are things I have seen that I will never forget, that will never go away."

He looked back at the lake. A short time ago, his face had been animated with the Thunderbird legend, now it reflected a private pain. Jamie waited, watching the plumes of vapor from his breath vanish into the cold air.

"I will never forget the day my mother died," Gray Feather said.

"How did it happen?"

Gray Feather sighed and rubbed the palms of his hands across his legs. "You could say that she died of sorrow. She was strong and full of spirit when my father was with us."

"Why did he leave?"

"He did not say. He was just gone. We had little food and scarcely enough firewood to heat the cabin for a week. He took what little money there had been. But like the lumberjack stealing the boots, that is not the worst thing he took."

Jamie looked at Gray Feather. "What, then? Did he take your ma's jewelry, a family treasure?"

"No, much worse. He took her spirit. Mother told me he had gone hunting or searching for work and that he would send for us. But the days turned into weeks, then months. We would have starved had it not been for the Sisters."

"Perhaps a bear got him...or wolves," Jamie said.

"Grandfather bear sleeps in the winter, and even a hungry pack of wolves will not attack a man."

"Still, the land is harsh; perhaps he got injured or sick and could not make it back."

Gray Feather shook his head. "Then they wanted our land."

"Who?"

"The lumber barons. Our land held fine timber. There was little an Indian woman and her half-breed son could do to stop their greed. They burned us out in the dead of winter. We were forced to seek shelter with the nuns. Mother became sick. With her spirit lost, she slipped away."

The two boys were silent for a moment. Jamie stole a glance at Gray Feather, his face stern, jaw set; a tear escaped and fled down his cheek.

"I will find my father someday."

"Why do you want to find him—if he left you and your mother to starve?"

"To kill him." His tone sent a chill through Jamie.

A deafening silence hung in the air then a roar grew within Jamie's head.

Close the sluice gate! The voice boomed in Jamie's head. The river was churning, unrelenting as it tumbled and hurled its way through the gate.

"I—I killed my father," Jamie said. He felt his voice crack; he swallowed hard. Gray Feather looked at him.

The Home Wind

Help me, boy! I can't do it alone. Pete. He must help Pete. But he was too weak. His legs wouldn't move. He tried to reach, but his arms were shriveled and useless.

"Jamie?"

The water was all around, logs everywhere, rising above him like a huge wall, hovering, ready to come crashing down…

"Jamie!"

Jamie snapped rigid. He blinked, momentarily lost to his surroundings. The river was gone.

"Are you all right, my friend?"

Jamie stood, legs trembling, his rump numb from the cold that had seeped through the blanket. He nodded.

"You must tell me the story that has caused you this unhappiness. Who is it that you killed?"

Jamie shook his head, not trusting his voice.

Gray Feather stood and put his hand on Jamie's shoulder. "When you are ready, my friend, I will be here to listen. You must release the *Mit-chi Man-i-tou*."

"What is…mitchy mana man, ah…"

"*Mit-chi Man-i-tou*. It is the spirit of evil."

An evil spirit—locked inside, thought Jamie.

"Do not wait too long to release it," Gray Feather said, "or there will be room for nothing else."

CHAPTER SEVEN
Babe And The Stray Dog

"I don't want those two boys going alone. I will not hear of it!"

Ma's voice shrilled through the trees. Jamie and Gray Feather halted their horses and looked at one another.

"What is Ma yelling about? She must be outside. Can you see her?" Jamie said. Gray Feather shook his head.

A second voice boomed. Jamie's horse pricked his ears. It was the foreman, Tom Haskins.

"I can't spare Pete and Ollie's busted up. I wouldn't trust any of the other jacks with my dirty socks. I sure can't send that Indian boy alone. I got little use for him but I don't want some soused-up jack stealing the camp money or the provisions."

The distorted voices filtered through the woods. The pitch of Jamie's mother's voice intensified.

"What makes you think the same drunken fool wouldn't beat up and steal from my son?"

"White boy. Most will think he lives in town and won't have enough cash to buy a stick of peppermint. Besides, robbing a white boy could land a jack in the pokey."

"And what's to stop these godless souls that frequent Seney from molesting Charlie when he's with James?"

"Indian helper. Lots of them around. They'll figure the Indian goes with your boy and that your boy's got a pa around. Kind of like the difference between a stray dog and one that's got a master. Most men won't mess with a dog that's got a master. Throw stones, just for fun, at a stray."

"I am not a stray dog," Gray Feather said.

"Shhh. I think Haskins is winning. Just think Gray Feather," Jamie whispered, "we might be goin' to Seney! Why, I have heard so many stories of that town. Did you know there are dozens of saloons? And there are women who walk around all day in their underdrawers!"

Haskins voice cut in. "Your boy's goin' to be a man soon. Got to turn him loose some time, Ma'am."

"The town is ripe with sin! Why the folks who live there hide their womenfolk and children when the lumberjacks come into town." Ma's voice pierced the air.

"That's mostly tall tales. It's just Saturday nights that are bad. Tomorrow's Wednesday. Town's quiet on Wednesday, 'cept for a stray jack or two that never made it back to camp."

"I don't know. James has not had much experience. He's a babe in the woods." Jamie heard Gray Feather snicker.

"At least I'm not a stray dog," Jamie snapped.

Gray Feather held a finger to his lips for silence.

"Look, Ma'am, grub's not goin' to hold out much longer. We need some meat besides game and sowbelly, and tea and coffee. Could use some 'taters and whatever else's left in town. You're a good cook, Missus, but you need the provisions and I can tell you from experience that when their bellies are rumblin', the men can be grumpy as a bear comin' out of hibernation. The felling and stackin' will be done soon, but we got the river hogs to feed when we set up the wanagan for the spring drive."

"Yes, I know—it's just—if anything happened to James, I...I just couldn't bear...couldn't bear to lose him too."

"I guarantee his safety, Missus. Boy will be fine."

Jamie's mother was speaking, but her voice was lower and the boys could not make out the words.

"Darn, I can't hear," Jamie said.

"Your mother is agreeing. She is reluctant, but she is agreeing," Gray Feather said.

"But how... you can't make out the words?"

"No, but it is the voice of her words that tells me. Sometimes words have no meaning. Your mother, she wants to keep you here, safe, but she knows you must become like *Kwa-sind* to live in this place."

"What is...*Kwa-sind*?" Jamie said.

"A strong man," Gray Feather replied.

"Yes, *Kwa-sind*. Not some babe in the woods. But you can tell all that from my ma's voice?"

"Yes, her voice, and other things."

"What other things?"

Gray Feather shook his head. "Not now, my friend. This would be a great adventure for you. A trip to Seney! I would be honored to go with you." He laughed. "But I am not your dog."

"No—no, you are my friend. My true friend," Jamie said.

"The talking has stopped. Our fate is decided," Gray Feather said.

The two boys smiled at one another and nudged their horses to step out.

A tingle ran through Jamie and his cheeks flushed with anticipation.

The Home Wind

_____

"And remember your ciphering, James, when you go to the mercantile for your purchases. Some folks are not honest." Ma was lecturing and Jamie nodded. He forced a solemn expression on his face, though inside he was bursting with excitement.

Haskins poked at Gray Feather's shoulder and glared down at the Indian. "Don't be gettin' any smart ideas, boy, or I'll sic the Indian Bureau on you so fast you won't know what hit you—that's after I skin you alive."

Gray Feather's gaze was unblinking. He did not yield to the foreman's bullying and stood his ground. Jamie was afraid his friend would knock Haskins' poking finger away and ruin the whole trip.

Easy, thought Jamie.

"You Indians are all alike: born thieves. Just remember, I got my eye on you," Haskins continued.

"And mine on you," Gray Feather said.

Easy!

"What kinda sass is that?" Haskins said.

"There are some—unfortunate ladies who live there," Jamie's mother cut in.

Gray Feather and Haskins glared at one another. Haskins pulled his gaze away. An unspoken victory for Gray Feather.

"James, are you listening?" Ma scolded.

"Yes, Ma. There are some poor ladies. Are they beggars? Should we give them some food?"

"Well—not exactly," she said, faltering. "Do you remember Jezebel? In the Bible?" Jamie thought a minute, his mind scrambling through the dozens of Bible stories.

"Harlots," Gray Feather supplied.

It was coming back to Jamie—a vague suggestion of impropriety. His face brightened.

"The women in their underdrawers!" he shouted, triumphant.

"Oh Lord!" shouted his ma, throwing her hands heavenward.

"I will keep him clear of the Jezebels, Mrs. Kangas," Gray Feather said, "and the scallywags and rascals and swindlers and drunkards."

"Oh Lord!" Ma repeated.

Oh no, Jamie thought. The whole thing will be ruined! Frantically he glanced at Gray Feather and drew a finger across his throat.

Gray Feather nodded.

"I have been to Seney, Mrs. Kangas, and Tom Haskins is correct. It is quiet and full of church-going folks most of the time. The stories of streets being lined with saloons, why they are not true. There are churches and shops and homes, just like any town."

Jamie's ma calmed a bit. "I was there too," she said, "but it was before all the lumberjacks came. It's just that I've heard so many bad things."

"All fabrications," said Tom Haskins.

"Oh James, Charlie, please be careful," Ma said.

"We will, Ma. And I'll have Charlie, here. It's only for one night. What could happen?"

"I don't want to think about it. Oh Lord help me," Ma said, turning and going back to the cook shack.

The Home Wind

Jamie and Gray Feather looked at Haskins.

"I'll give you the greenbacks in the morning," Haskins said.

"You'll start at daylight. It's an easy trip. Head south along the tote road. Keep the Fox River to your left. You'll each need a horse plus an extra for bringing supplies back. Jamie, your ma's got a list. You'll be staying at the White House Hotel. It's the only respectable place in town. That'll cost you around two bits. The Indian can sleep with the horses at the livery probably no extra charge. Both of you take some grub. Company's not paying for any high-priced restaurant meals."

All this talk of money and hotels and restaurants was making Jamie's head spin. He hoped he could remember his arithmetic.

"And remember," Haskins added, setting his gaze on Gray Feather, "I got my eye on you."

Haskins turned on his heel and strutted off.

"*Ken-a-beek*", Gray Feather spat.

He looked at Jamie, jaw clenched. I will tell you the story of *Ken-a-beek*, the serpent, during our journey. It is not so different from your story of Noah's Ark."

Jamie nodded, unsettled by the venom in Gray Feather's voice. Yes, not the words, as Gray Feather had said, but the voice.

CHAPTER EIGHT
Seney

The horses stumbled along the rutted tote road that wound its way toward Seney. The sun had cut through the gray sky, allowing slashes of blue to poke through. The warmth of the sun soaked into Jamie's bones and turned the snow along the road into slush.

"The Moon of Bright Nights is very near," Gray Feather said, turning his face to the sun.

"What is that?" Jamie asked.

"It is your month of April."

"We call it mud season."

Gray Feather smiled. "You must think of things more like the Ojibwa then you can live in harmony rather than in battle with the land."

But springtime held no harmony for Jamie. For it was nearly a year ago in April—the Moon of Bright Nights as Gray Feather called it—that the river had claimed his father's life. Yet his father had spoken much like Gray Feather, feeling the spirit of the land, speaking of the trees as if they had a soul.

"I think the town is very near," Gray Feather said, breaking into Jamie's thoughts.

Images of his father faded as Jamie's excitement rose. He glanced over at Gray Feather and they exchanged a smile. From a distance, Gray Feather could pass as a white boy. His hair had been shorn to a respectable length by Jamie's ma. The Indian was clad in a pair of woolen jack pants, the cuffs hacked off by an axe and tucked into his boots. He had also been issued a flannel shirt and Mackinaw coat.

"There—across the stump field," Gray Feather said, pointing.

Jamie stood in his stirrups, straining to see the town through the brush and discarded treetops strewn across the stump field. He could make out the silhouette of a few innocuous- looking buildings. He had expected something more spectacular.

As they entered Seney the horses' ears swiveled to and fro homing in on the town's activities. Jamie's horse pranced with excitement and snorted at the unfamiliar sights, smells and noises of town.

"Welcome to Seney, my friend," Gray Feather said.

Jamie's head pivoted as he gawked at the buildings that flanked the street. At first glance, the establishments had a look of sameness about them, each sporting a weathered, worn look that blended with the gray winter landscape. But splashes of color soon emerged in the haphazard array of storefront and saloon signs with such names such as Red Eye Jack's and Pine Stump Saloon. The stories were true! Saloons everywhere, though there was a respectable sprinkling of shops and dry good stores as well. A church sat at the end of the street, its steeple commanding reverence over the seedy town. The churchyard and town cemetery abutted a weedy lot that held a rude structure, which bore a sign: Seney School. Likely that was where the town children were hunched over their primers.

People scurried along the boardwalk, its planks scarred and pocked from the lumberjack's hobnailed boots. Most seemed like ordinary folks, families and shopkeepers, all intent on their daily errands.

Jamie watched an elegant lady wrapped in a fur cape carrying an ermine muff bustle along the town boardwalk. She was escorted by a frock-coated gentleman who twirled a cane expertly. Jamie had never seen so fine a couple. Where were the ladies in their underdrawers? This was not at all what Jamie had expected.

"That is a lumber baron and his wife," Gray Feather said.

Jamie nodded and watched them strut. The door to Red Eye Jack's crashed open in front of the elegant couple. The woman gasped, stepping back. The baron placed a protective arm around the woman. A disheveled form staggered from the doorway, his progress hastened by a burly man sporting a drooping, walrus moustache. The burly man, likely the proprietor, had a firm grasp on the unfortunate man's Mackinaw as well as the seat of his pants. With a powerful hoist, the hapless figure lurched into the slushy street and fell dangerously close to the hooves of Jamie's horse.

"When will you shanty boys learn two bits won't buy what you want? When you got two dollars in your pocket then you can buy you a girl," shouted the saloonkeeper, hands on hips, his great moustache huffing with each word. A woman appeared next to him. Jamie caught a glimpse of her bobbing crown of red hair.

The fur-clad lady and her gentleman fled the scene as if confronted with the plague. Jamie and Gray Feather watched the rejected lumberjack struggle to his feet.

67

The Home Wind

"Blazes to you, Red Eye," he wailed, shaking his fist at the saloonkeeper who had shoved the red-headed lady back inside and slammed the door. "You won't be robbin' my pockets come spring." The jack turned to look at Jamie and Gray Feather. Blood trickled from the man's battered face, coming to rest somewhere within the unkempt beard.

"What are you lookin' at?" he snarled.

"Oh, nothing sir...ah..." Jamie stuttered.

"We are looking for the supply store," Gray Feather added.

"Go to blazes," the jack shouted.

Jamie and Gray Feather reined their horses around the man.

"Ah, now, supplies you say?" said the jack, stroking his crusty beard. He lifted his finger to the oozing wound on his forehead and winced.

"Say now boys, don't be scurrying off. I can help you get yer supplies."

"Oh, thank you sir. If you would just point us in the direction," Jamie said.

"No, no lads. Why you look as if you've had a long trip. From a camp, I suspect. Now, I have a proposition for you."

Jamie and Gray Feather nudged their horses closer to the man.

"Now lads, why don't you just leave it to your old Uncle Harry to stock you up? I'll need your cash and list, boys then we can meet up somewhere."

Jamie's hand went to the wad of bills that his mother had sewn into the hem of his Mackinaw. The man's eyes followed his movement.

"Yessirree. Why you there remind me of my nephew. Why don't you just hand them greenbacks over to your ol' Uncle Harry and we'll meet yonder at the churchyard," the man said, jerking his head toward the church.

"Your offer is most kind," said Gray Feather, "however..."

"Shut yer maw, Indian. I'm talking to the boy, here."

Jamie thought of his Uncle Malcolm back East. This man who wavered like ragweed in the wind did not resemble Uncle Malcolm.

"Shifty," whispered Gray Feather out of the side of his mouth.

"Now I told you to shut yer yap," said the man poking a shaking finger at Gray Feather. The man grabbed the bridle of Jamie's horse.

"Now hand over them bills, boy. I see where you got 'em hid. Oldest place in the book, hem of yer coat."

Jamie jerked the reins and his horse pulled free from the man's grasp. The boys dug their heels in, pivoting their horses, and lunged away. The pack horse, its lead line snapping taut, scrambled for footing slinging clumps of frozen dirt and slush onto the man. Jamie could not make out the lumberjack's words, but he had a notion the fellow was not bidding them a pleasant stay in Seney.

Once safely away, the boys slowed their horses and began their search for a place to fill their list. Jamie's stomach rumbled and his rump was sore from the long ride. A wonderful aroma wafted through a doorway where people were entering. "Maggie's Eatery," stated a neatly lettered sign.

The Home Wind

"This must be a one of those restaurants that Tom Haskins told us he wouldn't pay for," Jamie said. "Ma gave me some coins, though. You think we should?"

The two boys halted in front of the eatery and stared at the door. It opened again and a man stepped out. He glanced at them.

"Best food in town, boys," he said, picking at his teeth with a splinter of wood.

Jamie and Gray Feather glanced at one another then dismounted. They tied their horses to a railing and moved toward the door. Jamie opened it a crack, peeking in. The pleasant smells assaulted him, bringing a long, low rumble from his stomach.

"Well come on in and shut the door. You'll be letting all the heat out."

A plump woman motioned them into a room that held many small tables, rather than one long one like at the lumber camp. Gray Feather glanced around, shrinking into his clothing.

"Some places don't want Indians," he hissed.

"Well this ain't one of them places," the woman said. Jamie stared into her strong, broad face. Dark, shiny braids coiled mysteriously into a coronet on top of her head. She scowled at the boys, deepening the furrows on her brow and pointed at a table.

"She is one of us," Gray Feather whispered.

"What?"

"She is an Indian!"

"Oh."

"Where you young 'uns from? Ain't seen you around."

"Wha—oh, we're not from town. Ah, we're from up river at the lumber camp, Ma'am," Jamie said.

"Name's Maggie. Couple of errand boys, eh?"

"Yes 'um, ah, Miss Maggie," Jamie said.

The woman grunted and put her fists on her ample hips. "So what you boys want? Stew's good. Otherwise, I got some eggs and can fry up some 'taters."

"Stew's fine with me, how 'bout you Gray, er, Charlie?"

Gray Feather nodded. "Stew."

Maggie grunted again, spun on her heel and disappeared into another room.

Jamie looked around the room. There were several other people in the restaurant. Two men stared at the boys. Jamie remembered his hat and snatched it off his head. Gray Feather left his on trying to hide beneath it.

Maggie soon reappeared and slammed two plates of steaming stew in front of the boys, causing Jamie to jump. She left and returned again with a plate of bread.

"You got money, don' cha?"

Jamie nodded, "Yes Ma'am."

"Good," she barked, fists again buried in her hips. "Lick those plates clean and I'll give you a bowl of Maggie's famous prune whip."

Jamie stared at his plate. He could not imagine it being proper to lick his plate, so he picked up a fork and dug in.

"It is not as good as your mother's," whispered Gray Feather. "What is prune whip?"

Conditioned to silence during mealtime, Jamie shook his head and continued to shovel the food in.

The Home Wind

After every drop of gravy had been sopped up by their bread, Maggie reappeared and plunked down a frothy offering in front of each boy. They took small bites, testing the concoction on their tongues. It was surprising and sweet, better than cookies, the foamy topping melting on their tongues. Below that, the boys savored the pulpy sweetness of the prunes. The treats disappeared with a few shameless mouthfuls.

"You must tell your mother to make this prune whip," Gray Feather said.

Jamie nodded, licking the last remnants of sugar from his spoon.

"Had yer fill boys?" Maggie said.

She was extremely light of foot for such a large woman and seemed to appear out of nowhere to loom over the boys.

Jamie and Gray Feather nodded.

"That'll be two bits."

Jamie reached into his pocket and pulled out a handful of coins, which he presented to Maggie.

She clucked her tongue in disgust.

"Didn't yer pappy teach you any better? Now two bits is a quarter—that's the big one. Don't be showing folks all of your money. Won't last long in this town."

Their bill settled and bellies full, the boys left the warmth of the restaurant and stepped out into the darkening street.

"We must hurry to buy our supplies then buy some oats and hay for the horses," said Gray Feather. "Excuse me sir," said Gray Feather to a passing man, "could you tell us where we could purchase some provisions?"

Jamie stared at his friend. Such fancy language!

The man pointed across the street. "Over there—Baumgartner's. He'll fix you up. Better hurry, though," said the man. "Gonna close soon."

"Thank you, sir," Gray Feather said.

Jamie and Gray Feather untied the horses and hurried to the store named Baumgartner's. There, Gray Feather was not so welcome.

"Indian stays outside," said a man who stood behind a counter. "I can't watch him and wait on folks."

Jamie saw his friend's jaw tighten.

"I will be with the horses," Gray Feather said, "and the stray dogs."

Jamie felt panic rising. He was not sure he could carry the task through without his friend's help.

CHAPTER NINE
Baumgartner's

"So now what can I do for you, son?" said the man who must have been Baumgartner.

Jamie looked around the store, amazed at the variety of goods that surrounded him. He had never seen such a well-stocked larder. Cans of fruit and vegetables lined the shelves along with jams and jellies and tins of tea. The floor was heaped with burlap sacks of sugar, flour, coffee beans and cornmeal. Molasses and pickle barrels, sacks of potatoes, onions, kegs of nails and tables piled with bolts of cloth, blankets, boots, hats, and a few toys fought for space in the crowded store. The rustic plank counter that the shopkeeper leaned on was lined with jars of sweets, pickled eggs and hog joints, as well as pipe and chewing tobacco. There were even packets of seeds for planting a vegetable garden, though Jamie's ma said the growing season was too short there for most things.

"Goin' to be closing soon," Baumgartner said, his voice impatient.

"Oh, sorry, sir, it's just that..." Jamie pulled the crumpled list from his pocket and laid it on the counter. Baumgartner snatched it up.

The shopkeeper moved about the store filling the order, placing packages and bundles on the counter.

The Home Wind

"Indian can come in to fetch these things," Baumgartner muttered.

"Yes, sir," Jamie said. He moved to the door and motioned Gray Feather into the store. Gray Feather eyed Baumgartner who was hunched over a piece of paper where his stub of a pencil tallied up the bill. Gray Feather slid a package off the counter and carried it to the pack horse.

"I'm goin' to the shed to fetch the meat. You mind that Indian of yours don't get light fingers," Baumgartner said.

Gray Feather returned for another load. While lifting a sack of cornmeal off the counter, he glanced at the shopkeeper's tally sheet. He paused a moment, shifted the sack to the floor and picked up the tally sheet.

"He is trying to cheat us," Gray Feather said.

"What—how?" Jamie said.

"These numbers do not add up."

Jamie stared at the scratchy numbers on the tally sheet. "But, how can you tell?"

"Use your addition. Your mother has taught you, has she not?"

"Well, yeah, I guess," Jamie stuttered, wishing he had paid more attention.

"You must ask the man to re-add these figures."

"But, you should do it, you are better at arithmetic!"

"Yes, but he will never listen to me."

Jamie's heart pounded. He stared at the numbers. They seemed to laugh at him, mock him for his ignorance.

Baumgartner returned. "Meat's on the horse," he said, wiping his hands on his apron. Gray Feather entered again and slid another package off the counter. He nudged Jamie.

"Now, see here, sir, I think there has… is a mistake in your… I'm sure it is, ah, was an accident," Jamie stammered, his voice croaking like a bullfrog.

Gray Feather nodded and moved out the door with his bundle.

"What's that you say, boy?" Baumgartner said, staring over the top of his spectacles at Jamie.

"These numbers don't add up sir!" Jamie blurted.

"That so?" The shopkeeper licked the lead of his pencil and scratched more figures on the paper.

Gray Feather entered and smiled encouragement to his friend.

The shopkeeper rubbed his hand over his jaw, his face intense with concentration.

"Well, don't that beat all," Baumgartner said. "Boy must be paying attention in school. I did make a miscalculation of nearly two dollars." He shoved the newly figured scrawl toward Jamie who stared at the paper, pretending to add. Gray Feather sidled up to the counter, taking his time to hoist the last package. He looked at the new calculation and nodded.

"That's more like it," Jamie said. He slid his hand through a slit in his coat hem and removed a bundle of bills. He started to hand the bills over to the shopkeeper, who reached out expectantly. Then Jamie hesitated, looking at the wad of greenbacks. Carefully he peeled of bill after bill, his lips moving while he counted silently. He was remembering the lessons his mother had drilled into him! He glanced at the figure on the sheet again, put the remaining bills in his pocket, and pulled out some coins. The shopkeeper grunted and snatched the money off the counter.

The Home Wind

"Six peppermint sticks, also, please sir," said Jamie, sliding a nickel and penny across the counter.

Baumgartner motioned toward the jars of sweets. "Help yerself," he muttered. Jamie made his selection and strutted out the door.

"Good day, sir," Jamie said as the door slammed behind him. He turned, seeing Baumgartner's glaring face through the door glass for a moment before the shopkeeper jerked down the shade announcing that the store was closed.

Jamie and Gray Feather stared at one another for a moment.

"He was trying to cheat us," Jamie said, dumbfounded.

"Yes, but he did not get away with it. He feels very foolish, being caught red-handed by a boy," Gray Feather said.

"But, it was you who caught him. Without you, I wouldn't have had enough money left to stable the horses and pay for the hotel room. He would have taken it all for certain!"

"That is why I am here, to watch over you, my friend," Gray Feather said.

"But, it's not fair. He treated you like—like you were going to steal from him, but he tried to steal from us."

"Everyone will steal from you: The shopkeeper, the lumber company, the camp boss. It is best to trust no one."

"But I trust you, Gray Feather. And Ma and Pete. You trust me, don't you?"

Gray Feather looked at Jamie. "Yes, James. You I trust."

They mounted their horses. Jamie picked up the pack horse's lead rope.

He remembered the peppermint sticks. Laying the lead rope over his horse's withers, he pulled two candy sticks out of his pocket.

"Peppermint?" he said, offering one.

Gray Feather reached over and took the candy. He bit into it and chewed thoughtfully. "It sticks to my teeth."

"You're supposed to suck on it to make it last, not bite it."

Gray Feather shrugged and took another bite. "Why make it last?"

"Because it is good."

"Yes," Gray Feather said thoughtfully. "That is a good idea."

"So, what now?" Jamie asked.

Gray Feather pointed his peppermint stick down the street. "The livery is that way. At least that is what a man told me when I was loading the horse. We must bed down the horses and secure these goods in the stable. I will sleep there and watch the supplies. You must go to the hotel that I am told is near the livery."

Jamie and Gray Feather rode down the street. A strange feeling like hunger or thirst filled Jamie. Yet, something inside him was lost—gone forever. He felt empty, but it was not hunger he felt, for the meal at Minnie's Eatery was still with him. He was cold and tired but he felt that way every day as he served the men at the lumber camp. Fear? Maybe, but not the fear of coming face to face with a black bear in the thimbleberry patch and certainly not the terror that filled him at the sound of rushing water. It was vague, like the feeling that he was being followed. Were they being followed? Jamie turned and looked behind him, but the streets were nearly deserted. Shopkeepers were locking their doors. A thin melody floated through the air, perhaps coming from a saloon. No sinister figures lurked in the shadows. All seemed quiet in Seney.

CHAPTER TEN
Bartering

There was nothing to fear, Jamie told himself. He nudged his horse to catch up with Gray Feather and looked at his friend. As long as he had Gray Feather, he had someone besides Ma that he could trust. Jamie was confused about the unfounded mistrust total strangers showed toward Gray Feather just because he was an Indian.

"Here is the stable," Gray Feather said. They halted, dismounted and led their horses inside. There they found a man wearing a blacksmith apron forking hay into the mangers of several horses. A lantern light cast a yellow glow throughout the stable.

"You must bargain with the man," Gray Feather whispered. "Tell him you only have fifty cents to feed and bed the horses."

The man stopped and looked expectantly at them.

"We need to put our horses up for the night," Jamie said.

"Put 'em over there," the man motioned with his hay fork at some empty stalls. "That'll be seventy-five cents for the three horses, in advance. If your Indian's staying here that's another two bits."

"I only have fifty cents," Jamie said matter-of-factly.

"Then I guess one of the horses don't get to stay," said the man. He looked at Jamie, sizing him up.

The Home Wind

Jamie splayed his legs, planting his feet as he had seen the jacks do. "I will pay you seventy-five cents for the three horses and my friend, Charlie Gray Feather," Jamie said.

"Thought you said you only had fifty cents," the man said, squinting one eye at Jamie.

"I was saving twenty-five cents to purchase some medicine for my ailing mother—not that it's any of your affair," Jamie said, crossing his arms and squinting back at the man.

"Ailing ma, huh? What's wrong with 'er?"

"Ah...it's ah," Jamie stammered.

"The consumption," offered Gray Feather.

The man sniffed as though he smelled something gone bad then sighed.

"Go ahead and save yer two bits fer yer sickly ma, then," he said, waving and arm in dismissal.

"Thank you, sir," Jamie said, handing the man a dollar bill.

"So, you been holding out on me. This here's a dollar. First you only got fifty cents then you got seventy-five, now it's a whole dollar."

"I'm going to be staying at the hotel."

The man let a smile slip as he took the dollar. He reached into his pocket and dug out change. "Name's Smithy. You staying at the White House?"

Jamie nodded.

"That quarter change ain't gonna buy you any kind of a room and your ma's medicine. But I reckon you've got another dollar or two stashed, don't ya boy?"

Jamie shrugged.

"Best lock your door or whatever you got won't be there in the morning," Smithy said.

Jamie and Gray Feather un-tacked and unloaded the horses and put them in the stalls.

The man forked hay into their mangers. "Oats over there," he said jerking his head toward a wooden bin.

Gray Feather measured out oats for the horses while Jamie carried buckets of water. Gray Feather spread a blanket over a mat of straw to make his bed.

"I'm goin' home to supper. I'll be around at daybreak," the man said.

"We will be gone at first light," Gray Feather said.

Smithy shrugged. "Keep an eye on them supplies, too, if I was you."

The man blew out the lantern leaving Jamie and Gray Feather in near darkness.

"Well, I guess I'll head over to that hotel unless you want me to stay here with you, that is," Jamie said.

"No, James. How often do you have a chance to sleep in a hotel in a real bed? Go, now, and get some sleep so that we can get an early start back to camp."

"All right. Well, g'night," Jamie said.

"Sleep well," Gray Feather said.

Jamie moved out of the stable into the nighttime shadows. The street slush, now frozen, crunched beneath his feet, the noise invading the still night. He stopped, getting his bearings, looking for the hotel. There, across the street. The saloon music had stopped. Footsteps, not his own, crackled somewhere behind him then stopped abruptly. He walked on, deliberately noisy then paused.

The Home Wind

The footsteps were still there, keeping pace. Jamie hurried, running and stumbling along the ruts of ice across the street to the boardwalk in front of the White House Hotel. He waited, listening. No footsteps. His breath, which he had been holding, came out with a rush. Heart pounding, he waited. Only silence. Jamie turned the doorknob and entered a small room warmed by a stove surrounded by a few dilapidated chairs.

"Hello—anybody here?" Jamie was beginning to wish he had stayed with Gray Feather in the stable. The empty hotel gave him the willies.

"I'm coming," someone hollered.

A stooped man leaning heavily on a cane, hobbled into the room. He stepped behind a crude counter and eyed Jamie as he approached.

"What do ya want?" the stooped man said.

"I'd like a room, please," Jamie said.

"You shanty boys know I'm off limits. Stay out of my hotel or I'll..."

"But, I—are there any rooms left? I mean if you're full and all . . ."

"Hoodlums! This here's the only respectable hotel. Don't want some lumberjack here dirtying the lobby up," said the old man. He lifted his cane and waved it menacingly at Jamie.

"Hoodlums, sir?" Jamie said, backing toward the door.

The old man lowered his cane and pulled a pair of spectacles out of his pocket and slipped them on. He squinted at Jamie.

"You're just a boy," he said.

"Yes sir."

"What you want a room for, then?"

"To sleep. I'm very tired, I . . ."

The old man bent under the counter and pulled out a book. He slammed down and opened it, thumbing through the pages. He shoved an ink pot and pen across the counter. "Why didn't you say so? Sign in. That'll be a dollar."

"A dollar! I was thinkin' maybe two bits!"

"For two bits you can sleep on the boardwalk."

"But I'm so tired and I only have a quarter," Jamie said, hearing the shrill whine that his mother hated.

"Oh, all right. Two bits then, since yer just a boy. But you won't be getting any sheets." Jamie slapped his quarter on the counter. The man need not know that he still had an extra dollar in the lining of his coat. He lifted the pen and dipped it in the pot of ink. As he tried to write, a large blot of ink smeared across the page.

The old man snatched the pen from him.

"Never mind. Here's yer key. End of the hall."

Jamie tried to wipe the excess ink from his hand before taking the key.

"Up them steps," said the old man, pointing with his cane. "Room number three."

Jamie hurried up the steps into the dimly-lit hallway. He found room three and tried the knob, but it wouldn't turn. Locked. He slipped the key into the hole and turned. The door swung open. He entered and re-locked the door, fumbling in the dim light. Jamie found a lamp and matches on a table, lit the lamp, and surveyed his room. It contained an iron bedstead, mattress with yellowish stuffing coming out, wash basin, and a chamber pot tucked beneath the bed. Something scurried across the floor, causing Jamie to jump. A tiny fireplace sat cold as granite and the wood box was empty. He might as well be in the barn! Jamie approached the bed and lay tentatively across the stained and lumpy mattress. The bedsprings screeched in protest. He pulled up a moth-eaten blanket from the foot of the bed. It smelled musty. He had not bothered to remove his boots, for it was far too cold in the room to take anything off.

Jamie sighed and turned on his side, trying to get comfortable. Something poked him in the ribs. Off-the-floor beds were highly overrated, Jamie decided. How he wished he had stayed with Gray Feather. It was going to be a long, cold night.

CHAPTER ELEVEN
The Thief

When Jamie awoke, his head was thick from a bad night's sleep. He was momentarily disoriented in the unfamiliar surroundings. Slowly the events of the past day returned to him as he sat up and surveyed the hotel room, now even more derelict in the sunlight. The sun was up! Never could he remember sleeping until the sun rose. Why hadn't Gray Feather fetched him? They would have to hurry to return to the lumber camp before dark. There would be no time to wash up or have a hot breakfast, though Jamie had no idea where to get water for washing anyway and he was reluctant to spend any of his precious remaining dollar on a return visit to Maggie's Eatery. A few left-over stale biscuits would have to suffice.

Jamie could not, however, ignore the urgency to find a privy. But where? Then he remembered the chamber pot poking from beneath his bed. After relieving himself, Jamie wondered if he was expected to empty the thing. But where—how? Jamie carefully shoved the vessel back under the bed. He would be long gone before the ornery proprietor would discover this transgression.

Jamie stumbled down the stairway, feeling like he'd been used to mop the floors. He passed the crude desk in the hotel entry and was grateful that the old man was not there. Jamie smoothed his hair before jamming his hat on and stepping into the brace of fresh air. He gulped it in, trying to rid himself of the stale feeling from the hotel. Quickly Jamie made his way to the stable. The man who called himself Smithy was mucking out the stalls. Jamie stopped as if smacked by a blow, his mouth gaping. The empty stalls—the ones that his and Gray Feather's horses had occupied! Jamie relaxed a minute. Of course, Gray Feather must have the horses out back, bridled, packed and ready to go.

Smithy paused from his work and looked at Jamie.

"Gray—I mean Charlie Gray Feather, my friend, the Indian, is he out back?"

"No," Smithy said, his voice carrying a question.

"But, where, how..." Jamie felt panic prickling his neck.

"Neither hide nor hair of your Indian or the nags when I got here at daybreak," Smithy said.

Jamie rushed outside the stable, running out back. There were multiple hoof prints in the snow. A sack lay in a crusty drift, its contents of cornmeal spilling from a tear. Jamie inspected the bag, trying to think, trying to control his growing fear. Where was Gray Feather? He tried to push the impossible thought away. Gray Feather would not have left without saying anything. He would never steal from Jamie. Never! Yet, the horses and the grub were gone. Vanished! Jamie stumbled to the side of the stable. Firewood was piled under the stable overhang; an axe lay in the snow—and blood! Jamie dropped to his knees and inspected the blood. But it couldn't be Gray Feather's. If someone had killed him, they would have left him there. Where was the body? Maybe he was hurt! Maybe he had crawled off to die. Maybe he planted the blood, beheading some hapless chicken to make it look like he had been hurt. But Jamie was certain, positive his friend would never betray him.

Jamie knelt in the snow, his breathing coming in quick gasps. He touched the spattered pattern of blood.

"Always said you couldn't trust no Indian."

Jamie jumped to his feet and reeled around to see Smithy standing at the corner of the stable, his arms crossed in front of him.

"Looks like your thieving Chippewa skedaddled with your horses and your supplies. That there blood's from last night's goose supper."

Jamie didn't know whether to be relieved or enraged. He was relieved that Gray Feather had not met the business end of the axe, but doubt was beginning to peck at him like a crow at a carcass.

Jamie stood and brushed the clumps of snow from his knees. He looked at Smithy. "Gray Feather would never steal from me. We are friends, like—like brothers."

Smithy laughed. He pointed at the snow. "Hoof prints lead off that way. If you're from the Fox River camp, that's the other direction. Never knew an Indian didn't know his directions. Sorry to tell you boy, your Indian friend will have them goods peddled off before you can spit."

Jamie studied the hoof prints and began following them.

"Where you going boy! You can't track that Indian, least not without snowshoes. Still four feet of snow in places."

"Then lend me some snowshoes! I'll return them."

The Smithy went into the stable and returned with a set of bear-paw snowshoes.

The Home Wind

"This ain't no loan. This here's a rental. That'll be a dollar."

"A dollar! Why I could buy a pair of these for less than a dollar!" Jamie cried.

"Okay, then. These here are yours for a dollar. You drive a hard bargain boy."

"But I don't want to buy them, I just want to borrow them."

"I don't loan my equipment. I'm a businessman. I either rent my goods or I sell 'em." Jamie sighed and dug his last dollar from the lining of his coat and handed it to Smithy.

Any thoughts of Seney being gilded with glamour and adventure had long faded. This blasted town could go straight to the devil.

He strapped on the snowshoes and followed the hoof prints. Soon he noticed something odd. It was evident that two of the horses were traveling together, tandem, as if a rider leading the pack animal behind. But the third horse was making its own trail, parallel with the other, too far away to have been led by the rider. Jamie quickened his pace.

"I knew it!" he said out loud. "Gray Feather did not steal from me! He is following the man who did."

Jamie huffed loudly as he hurried along, his snowshoes leaving their pattern over the hoof prints. He could see that the horses were floundering at times. It would be rough going, traveling off the tote roads. The snow had melted and refrozen, forming a crust that their hooves would break through. However, his snowshoes sunk very little, rarely penetrating the snow crust. Jamie stopped a moment, listening. All was quiet except for his labored breathing. He felt the dampness beneath his layers of clothing. Must be careful, he thought, or I'll freeze when the sweat begins to dry. Jamie settled his straddled pace into a rhythm. He was making good time, without exhausting himself. Soon his breathing slowed and regulated.

He followed the trail. The crunching of his steps sounded a beat, like a song his mother had taught him. He entered a woods. Monster pines still untouched by the crosscut saw loomed around him, cutting the warmth of the sun and casting dark shadows across the trail. They were magnificent, these few that remained. Still, he missed the warmth of the sun, and the openness of the stump field he had traversed. In the woods, where the remaining white pine humbled him, he felt uneasy. The wind hushed through the pines in a ghostly whisper. *That is their soul you feel, their voice, singing, their spirit calling you, son.* His father's words, sometimes so much like Gray Feather's, filled his head.

He began humming, trying to sing with the pine, his voice a tuneless cadence. "Oh, where have you been, Billy Boy, Billy Boy?"

He stopped, studying the trail. Why had Gray Feather veered off? Clearly the single horse had cut off, the two trails forming a wavering Y through the trees. The brave choice would have been to follow the two horses. Yet, he must find Gray Feather, he reasoned. His friend would know what to do.

"OOOHHHH where have you been, charming Billy?" Jamie bleated.

The Home Wind

The snow was not crusty in the woods, and deeper. He followed the single-horse trail, his voice rising with his effort to summit a large drift. "I HAVE BEEN TO SEE THE WIFE, SHE'S THE JO-OY OF MY LIFE, SHE'S A YOUNG THING AND CANNOT LEAVE HER MOTHER!"

His snowshoes threatened to slide backwards. Jamie reached forward to grab a branch for leverage when something someone seized him from behind forcing his face into the drift, his snowshoes shooting out from under him.

"Ooof," Jamie grunted, the wind being forced from him.

He squirmed beneath the weight of his attacker, the snowshoes making it impossible to get his feet beneath him. A hand clapped over Jamie's mouth, stifling any cries for help.

"Quiet, my friend. It is only me."

Gray Feather? It was Gray Feather! Jamie pulled Gray Feather's hand from his mouth and rolled to his side, causing the Indian to tumble down the snowdrift.

"Gray Feather!" Jamie yelped.

"Quiet, James," Gray Feather hissed. "He is very near."

Jamie placed his own hand over his mouth, angry at his own stupidity. Voices carry in the winter woods like thunder over the lake. Jamie sat then rose to his feet. He reached out to pull Gray Feather up.

"I am sorry if I frightened you, my friend, but I had to quiet that *e-wa-yea*," Gray Feather whispered.

"What's an *e-wa-yea*?"

"A song, like one's mother would sing to her papoose."

"What!" Jamie shouted.

Gray Feather held his finger to his lips.

Jamie clapped his hand over his mouth again, then quickly pulled it away. Remembering to whisper, he said, "Where is your horse?"

"I have tied him over there," Gray Feather pointed. "I do not want him greeting his horse friends as we draw near. The man who calls himself Uncle Harry is over that way." Gray Feather pointed off into the woods. "Do you smell the smoke from his fire?"

Jamie stared off into the trees. He could see nothing, smell nothing.

"But I do not understand, Gray Feather. How did he manage to steal the horses and supplies when you were right there with them?" Jamie said.

"I will explain later. We must go quietly, like the deer," Gray Feather said, his words hushed. "We must not talk." Jamie nodded.

"We will use hand signals."

Jamie nodded again.

Gray Feather pointed at Jamie's snowshoes and made motions with his hands.

Jamie removed the bear paws and they followed the two-horse trail; Jamie behind Gray Feather, imitating his moves, trying to move with stealth. Their footsteps fell silently in the soft snow. Soon Gray Feather held up his hand, signaling Jamie to stop. Gray Feather pointed. There, through the trees, blending with them stood a small log cabin. A thin curl of smoke rose from the chimney. The horses still tacked and loaded, were tethered to trees. Gray Feather made the signal to proceed. Willing silence, Jamie followed his friend, using trees as cover. Gray Feather gave Jamie a sign to stay, thrusting the palm of his hand toward him.

Jamie nodded and watched Gray Feather, crouched low, approach the cabin. Jamie held his breath, praying the man, the thief, would not choose the moment to look out of the cabin's tiny window when Gray Feather was peering in. Moving like a cat, Gray Feather moved from the cabin, past the watchful gaze of the horses, back to Jamie.

"He is sleeping inside the cabin," Gray Feather whispered. "He has many bottles around him." Gray Feather imitated drinking out of a bottle. "I think he got drunk and now he sleeps."

"What's our next move? Jamie said.

"We take back our boots, my friend."

"Huh?" Jamie said. Then he remembered Gray Feather saying that it was not so bad when a man stole your boots because you could steal them back. "But how?"

Gray Feather made a sign to follow and pointed toward the horses. He made motions with his hand.

"Huh? Oh," Jamie said. Untie the horses, he thought. He nodded. But what was Gray Feather going to do? Jamie moved toward the horses, certain the whole world could hear the thundering of his heart and the rasp of his breathing. He watched Gray Feather out of the corner of his eye. The Indian picked up a hefty branch, toted it to the cabin and slipped it against the door.

Jamie approached the horses and petted them. He untied their tethers and began leading them away. Gray Feather wedged the branch against the door of the cabin. Careful,

Gray Feather, Jamie thought. The branch might snap and make a noise. But Gray Feather succeeded and created an obstacle that would surely slow the thief, once aroused from his drunken slumber.

Jamie reached the spot where he had left his dollar snowshoes. He wasn't about to leave those behind, he thought as he tied them to the pack horse. Gray Feather, his task done, moved quickly to join Jamie. Gray Feather took the reins of one horse and made a pointing motion in the opposite direction of the cabin. Plowing through snowdrifts, the boys and horses moved off. Jamie heard a distant nicker. His horse nickered back. He placed his hand over the animal's muzzle. They made their way along a trough cut between the drifts until coming upon a thick stand of immature pines. Jamie could see the third horse through breaks in the branches. Gray Feather had put the horse's feed sack on, a clever way to muffle any noise.

"We have made it, James," Gray Feather, said. Jamie was annoyed that his friend's brow held not one bead of sweat, nor was he winded in the least. Jamie, on the other hand, was exhausted.

"We cannot make it back to camp before dark," Gray Feather said. "We should back track, to mislead Uncle Harry if he follows, but the horses are tired from breaking through so much snow."

Jamie nodded. It was true. The horses' coats were matted with dried sweat, their eyes dull and tired. Surely they were as thirsty and hungry as Jamie. "What do we do?" Jamie said.

"We will find the river," Gray Feather said.

The Home Wind

James was lost. He had no idea where the river was, had not bothered with remembering direction as he followed Gray Feather's trail.

"Then we will make camp and leave at first dawn. Remember, we kept the river to our left as we went to Seney. To return to camp, we must keep it to our right."

"But where is the river?" Jamie said.

"It is not far. We will let the horses' thirst find it for us."

Gray Feather led his horse from its hiding place and removed the feed sack.

"We will give you oats soon," Gray Feather said to the horse. "But first, you must take us to the river."

The boys mounted, Jamie picked up the reins and the lead rope of the pack horse. "Give him his head," Gray Feather said.

"But what if he spooks."

"He is too tired. Loosen the reins and give him freedom."

Jamie obeyed. His horse dropped his head, stretching its tired neck muscles. It turned to look at Jamie, as if waiting for instruction.

"To the river," Gray Feather said.

"Yes, take us to the river," Jamie repeated.

Jamie was surprised when the horse moved out, plodding with great purpose through the woods and into a stump field.

"You see, my friend, the river will always be abutted by the barren stump land, for your lumberjacks will cut the trees nearest the river where they must float them to the sawmill."

"That's true," Jamie said. "I never thought of that."

The sun was dipping close to the horizon as they moved on, reins slack. Jamie thought of his ma, wringing her hands with worry. They would have to concoct some story or she would never let him into the woods alone again. Gray Feather would think of something. He was the master of tales. Jamie turned and looked at his friend. Everything felt right now that Gray Feather and he were back together.

"I—I'm glad I found you again, Gray Feather," Jamie said.

"I knew you would, James. I left a trail even a blind man could follow. I knew you would figure it out when you found I had made a separate trail, even though it would have been much easier for my horse to follow the broken trail of the man called Uncle Harry."

Jamie felt a wave of pride wash over him. It was true, he did figure out Gray Feather's signal. Still, he was confused.

Jamie asked, "How did Uncle Harry steal horses and supplies right under your nose? Surely he must have had a lantern and you must have been awoken."

"Yes. I heard Uncle Harry. He made enough noise to awaken my long-dead ancestors. But he was carrying an axe. He stood over me, holding the axe up, ready to use it. I watched through an eye slit, pretending to sleep. I waited, barely daring to breathe, figuring when he brought it down I would roll out of the way. Then, well, I would slash him with my knife."

"But you didn't. Why?"

"The axe never came down. I pretended to sleep. Uncle Harry just shrugged and went about his business stealing two of our horses. He loaded them with our supplies. He did not pack things well because he was trying to hold on to the axe at the same time. He took the horses out back and I crawled after him, keeping in the shadows. He lost a sack of meal out back, which broke open. He finally dropped the axe in the snow, mounted up and rode off. I tacked up the other horse and followed."

"Why didn't you stick him with your knife when you had the chance?" Jamie said.

"Because I did not have to and because I did not want to be punished for killing a white man."

"But, he was going to use an axe on you!" Jamie said.

Gray Feather looked at his friend. "No one would believe an Indian. Besides, he did not use the axe and I did not use my knife. It has worked out for the best."

"Why didn't you come and get me!" Jamie said.

"I tried, my friend. The door to the hotel was locked. I rapped a long time and finally an old man came. He carried a stick. He would not hear me out and swung the stick at me, missing me by inches."

Jamie nodded. The proprietor of the hotel did not exhibit much better behavior toward his paying customers.

"Do you hear the noise?" Gray Feather said.

"What noise?"

"The river, as it rushes."

Jamie could hear it. It was growing louder with each step the horses took. But it was frozen when they had left the lumber camp only yesterday morning. The warm sun had broken through the shell and the water, which had flowed silently beneath the ice, had burst free. Louder and louder it roared in Jamie's head. And the vision came of his father and the river and the log jam. And the sluice gate. But this time Jamie was not there—not at the sluice gate. The sound of his dream meshed with the real river, hypnotizing, carrying a beat that matched the stride of his horse. He could hear Gray Feather calling his name, commanding the release of *Mitchi Manitou*.

"We are here, James. The river."

And his father was gone as was the colossal long jam and the infamous sluice gate; only Jamie and Gray Feather and the horses facing the icy flow of the river.

The horses plunged their muzzles into the water, breaking away a thin layer of ice. Today the river held no death. Today the river was life. Jamie dismounted and crouched next to the river. He pushed away thin sheets of ice and dipped his hands into the numbing water, his thirst suddenly overpowering. He drank from his cupped hands then splashed his face. Yes, today it was life.

CHAPTER TWELVE
Burdens

Jamie and Gray Feather adjusted oat-filled feedbags over the horses' heads. There were more stale biscuits for the boys along with leathery pieces of jerky. Jamie's mouth watered at the thought of another frothy plate of prune whip. He eyed the sacks of provisions, wishing he knew how to transform flour into bread. They had eaten the remaining peppermint sticks during their journey. The sugar had made Jamie even hungrier.

Gray Feather was blowing on the initial sparks of a fire he had started. He had cut small shavings from sticks with his knife to make tinder. Jamie rummaged in a potato sack and withdrew a spud.

"I'm so hungry, I'm gonna to eat this raw," Jamie said.

Gray Feather nodded, his cheeks puffing as he blew life into the fire, now crackling softly. He added tiny sticks to the small tongue of flame.

Jamie took a bite into the gritty potato. He should have washed it in the river.

"I need more firewood, James, dry sticks—dead ones—break off the branches with no needles."

Jamie did as instructed. The sound of snapping branches cracked through the air. He foraged the bare patches of ground and produced a small armload of wood.

"More. We will need more or we will freeze."

The Home Wind

Jamie popped the last of the potato into his mouth and went about the chore of collecting firewood.

"Next we must build a shelter," Gray Feather said. "The entrance will be here, by the fire."

"How? It's almost dark," Jamie said.

"Now we need the boughs from the trees, still green so they will bend. We will make a mat on the snow then a roof over our heads. The white pine makes the softest mattress. Get the hatchet that I used to chop firewood for the larger branches.

Jamie and Gray Feather broke limbs from small pines and tucked them inside a copse of small trees.

"We will fill in the gaps of our roof with more limbs," Gray Feather announced, as he wove branches within branches.

The shelter was complete just as the final vestiges of daylight slipped away. Jamie added more wood to the fire.

"Not too much my friend."

"But I'm cold."

"Build a small fire and sit close. Then you can see your enemies approach."

"Do you think—Uncle Harry?"

Gray Feather shrugged. "He has no horse. He would be a fool to follow, but we must not let our guard down."

Jamie shivered.

"We have only the blankets from my bed roll I used in the stable," Gray Feather said. "We will sleep under them together. I hope you do not growl in your sleep like a bear."

Jamie laughed. He remembered Ma complaining of his pa's snoring. As if on cue, Jamie's stomach grumbled.

The boys laughed.

"Potatoes? Jamie asked.

"Yes, let's roast them in the fire."

They pulled two rutted potatoes from the sack and went to the river to wash them. The moon had risen and cast its reflection across the landscape. Jamie thought of the Thunderbird pulling the moon from the sky in anger. The boys skewered their potatoes on to sticks and dangled them over coals in the fire.

"Will you tell me another story, Gray Feather? Then it will not seem to take so long for the potatoes to roast. I know! You never told me about the serpent. I can't remember the name. You called Tom Haskins that name. It was, um..."

"*Ken-a-beek*," supplied Gray Feather.

"Yes! Tell me of *Kenabeek*."

Gray Feather poked at the coals beneath the potatoes sending sparks into the night air. "It is a story about a hero of many Ojibwa stories, *Nanobozho*."

"Tell me, please."

"One day, *Nanobozho* returned from a hunting trip and found that his friend was missing. 'Perhaps my friend has gone for a walk or to fetch water,' *Nanobozho* said, but then he saw the trail of the Great Serpent, *Kenabeek*, and he knew his friend had fallen to harm.

"*Nanobozho* set out to save his friend from the Great Serpent, crossing a great river, climbing mountains and traversing valleys until he came to the shore of a deep, dark lake called Manitou Lake—Spirit Lake—or the Lake of Devils. There the trail of the Great Serpent ended. I think the potatoes are getting burned."

The Home Wind

"Huh? Oh, yeah, I'm starved. But keep telling the story." Jamie tested the potato with his finger. "Ouch!"

"*Nanabozho* could see," Gray Feather continued, "at the bottom of the lake, the house of the Great Serpent. It was filled with evil spirits, *Mitchi Manitous* that were trapped like the one within you, my friend. They were guarding the horrible Serpent who was coiled around his friend, holding him prisoner."

Jamie blew on his potato. It was true. He could not make the dream go away, the vision of his pa being taken by the river and himself standing by, useless. But how to push it out? And what about Gray Feather? What about the evil he carried with him with his quest to kill his father? Jamie took a small bite of his potato.

"Burnt on the outside, raw in the middle. Just the way I like my supper," Jamie said.

Gray Feather stared at his own charred spud. "The head of the Serpent was blood-red, eyes glowing like the fire," he said pointing at the coals of the fire. He took a bite of his potato. "I have had worse, he said. Once I ate a raw mouse, fur and all. The tail was hard to chew."

Jamie stopped mid-bite and stared at Gray Feather.

"I was very hungry and there was not time to build a fire." Gray Feather smiled, a gleam in his eye.

"You're spoofin' me!" Jamie cried.

"...anyway, *Nanabozho* was not without his own powers, so he shouted to the sun, 'Come with all your strength and make the waters boil!' And the sun's heat bore down upon the evil lake and soon its waters churned and boiled, driving the Serpent and all the evil spirits from their lair.

But *Nanabozho's* friend still lay at the bottom of the lake. So *Nanabozho* called upon the west wind to blow on the lake and spread its waters so that his friend might be saved. And the wind came and it blew the lake with a fury and *Nanabozho's* friend escaped, free at last! But the water spread across the plains and valleys causing a great flood of all the land. Men, women and animals, in trying to escape the floods, quickly gathered timber for a raft. The water rose higher and higher until even the peaks of the mountains disappeared under the water."

"Noah's Ark!" Jamie shouted. "This is a story of Noah's Ark!"

"And when the water disappeared, the people and animals who survived learned that the Great Serpent had died. However, the evil spirits had returned to the bottom of the evil lake, waiting for another victim."

"That's the end? The evil spirits are there, waiting!"

Gray Feather nodded and added a stick to the fire. The flames licked hungrily around the new fuel. "It is like any enemy, it must be defeated. Only then will the burden be taken from you."

Jamie again thought of his burden and Gray Feather's. Each carried the burden of his father like a heavy rucksack.

"I am ready to sleep," Gray Feather announced. He crawled into the pine-bough shelter and arranged the blankets. Jamie followed. The boys lay beneath the Hudson Bay blankets, sharing each other's warmth. Jamie squirmed, searching for comfort atop the mat of branches. He felt as if his life had ended with his father's death then reawakened with Gray Feather. Jamie could not imagine

The Home Wind

his life without his friend. Fear crept up like the cold. What if he were to lose him, too? Jamie could not bear the thought.

"Spring is almost here," Jamie said.

Gray Feather grunted and turned on his side, pulling the blankets with him. Jamie pulled his share back.

"But you will not go! Where would you look next, anyway? There are too many camps and sawmills and towns. You will never find your father," Jamie said. "Besides, even if you did, how will you kill him. They will put you in jail or back at the Indian orphanage if you kill him. What is his name? You never told me his name."

"I will find him. His name is Angus MacGregor. You have more than your share of the blanket. Why all this talk?"

"Because, you—you can't go. Please don't go, Gray Feather! Stay with the camp, stay through the river drive. Then the scouts will go out looking for fresh timber. And the jacks will regroup, just like last fall. You can stay on as a chore boy with me. You can keep looking for your father."

Gray Feather shrugged. "Perhaps, if the camp moves west. I believe Angus MacGregor will move west where the distant timber stands untouched. It does not matter much where I go, until I get word of him—find a fresh trail leading to him."

The boys were quiet for a moment. But Jamie was nagged by this *Mitchi Manitou*, which seemed to be devouring Gray Feather.

Jamie asked," Why don't you let him go? Try to forget, like I try to forget?"

106

Gray Feather turned to face Jamie, but his features were dark and hidden. "You are not without wisdom, my friend. But some things cannot be forgotten or forgiven and must be destroyed or they will be the destroyer. Each must follow his own path. Mine will lead me to another camp, another town, as it led me to your camp, looking for the man, Angus MacGregor."

Gray Feather sat up and stared out of the shelter. "Now I am wide awake." He crawled to the edge of the shelter and put more wood on the fire. "I am waiting for my dreams to lead me to him. When I turned twelve, to the Ojibwa, I became a man. My father's actions cannot go unpunished and there is no one but me to see to his justice."

"But how? What will you do if—when you find him? I mean, how will you do it?" Jamie said. "Kill him, I mean."

"I do not know. This, too, will be brought to me at the right time."

Jamie nodded in the darkness and sighed. He had turned twelve the week before his pa had perished in the river. Soon he would be thirteen. To the Ojibwa he had been a man when he watched his father being swallowed by the river.

Gray Feather crawled back under the blankets. Jamie stared at a star whose light poked through a hole in the shelter roof. A wave of relief enfolded him. Gray Feather would stay, at least for a while. As the old worry ebbed, a new one crept in. Ma! She would be mad with worry. When Jamie and Gray Feather did finally arrive at the lumber camp, she would want to thrash them both for causing such distress.

"Gray Feather?"

The Indian sighed. "What?"

"What will we tell Ma?"

"The truth? We have done nothing wrong. We are bringing the supplies to camp, except for a few potatoes."

It was Jamie's turn to sigh. "But she was afraid something would go wrong, and it did. We have to tell her some reason for being late, or she'll never me out of her sight again."

"Yes, you are not yet a man in her eyes. She resists letting you become one. It is your turn, James, to tell a story. But do not worry. I'm sure you will think of a good, ah, story to tell her."

Jamie thought about the pathetic attempt at his last story after his ill-fated romp on the grand horse, Swede. She had seen through his feigned injury. He had forgotten which ankle. Jamie sighed and turned on his side, staring into the darkness. This would another fitful night's sleep.

CHAPTER THIRTEEN
Ma

Jamie and Gray Feather didn't dare push the tired horses beyond a walk. The going was difficult, as the tote road again turned into slush from the warming day. The packhorse had the most difficult job, carrying the shifting load of supplies. Dead weight, Jamie's father had said, is a much more difficult load to bear. Jamie felt himself nod off for a moment, nearly sending him tumbling off his horse before he jerked awake and righted himself. He glanced at Gray Feather who sat straight and alert. Is he human? Jamie wondered. At last the landscape became vaguely familiar and the weary horses picked up their pace.

"We are near," Gray Feather stated simply.

"Glory be," Jamie muttered.

Entering camp, Jamie spotted his ma, her back to the boys, standing at the stable entrance. Pete was there, too, tacking up a horse. He turned to Jamie's ma and took her hand. She did not pull it away. Jamie halted his horse as did Gray Feather. They looked at one another. What did this mean—hand holding? Jamie's horse whinnied. Pete's horse whinnied back. Pete and Jamie's ma turned to see the boys. Ma rushed toward Jamie as he dismounted. She embraced him tightly.

"I was so afraid I had lost you too, James," she muttered.

Her arms felt strong and good around him and he returned the embrace.

The Home Wind

"I'm sorry we're late, Ma, we, ah, got delayed."

"No matter son, you're back, thank the Lord. Pete was just heading out to look for you. I was certain you had gotten robbed and murdered on the road. Pete told me you would be fine, especially with Charlie, but..."

"No, Ma, everything went fine. It just took longer and we got, well, lost."

Ma released him and held him at arm's length, looking him in the eye. Her gaze shifted to Gray Feather who was dismounting. "I'm surprised you would get lost with Charlie along."

Pete joined them. "Even Indians can get lost," he said. He reached out and patted Jamie on the shoulder. "You worried your ma sick. But you got the job done, boy. I'm proud of you— both of you."

Pete let his hand slide off Jamie's shoulder. Did the hand pause a moment on Ma's arm, before dropping away? Why was Ma allowing Pete to touch her? Wasn't it forbidden? She was a widow. Jamie's head was spinning. He was too exhausted to think.

Jamie and Gray Feather unloaded and un-tacked the horses, giving them a good rub down, then lots of hay, water and oats. Always tend to the horse first, son, Pa had lectured. Then see to your own comfort. More than anything Jamie wanted to stagger into his corner of the cook shack and collapse onto his bunk. Never again would he complain about his straw mattress. It would surely feel like a cloud from heaven! It seemed forever getting to that bed. But there were still chores; they never ceased.

Jamie stole a glance at his ma, bent over the stove as she fried meat for the men's supper. A lock of hair had slipped from the tight bun. Her face was tired, as usual, perhaps more than usual. Probably from the worry Jamie had caused. Yet, there was something different in her face that Jamie had not seen lately. A twinkle. The light that had gone out when Pa died was back. Though she still wore a black skirt, she had exchanged the plain dark blouse she had worn since Pa died with an almost-gay checkered one. And she was humming something, and it was not a hymn.

Jamie and Gray Feather went through the motions of serving the men their supper. Jamie was numb with exhaustion but relieved that Ma had not punished or even scolded him. She refilled Pete's coffee cup at least a half dozen times that night—a chore normally left for the boys. When the pies came, Pete's was personally delivered by Ma, the slice much larger than those of the other men. When Ma served Pete, the man next to him winked and jabbed him with a friendly elbow. Jamie heard whispers and a snicker, but Ma didn't seem to notice. A hot streak burned up Jamie's neck, flushing his cheeks, adding confusion to his exhaustion.

At last Jamie felt the warmth of his bed, smelled the wool of his own blanket. Yet, sleep did not come. Had it only been two days since he and Gray Feather had left for Seney? It seemed months . . . years! In two days, his ma had somehow changed. Not really changed to someone new, but had changed back. Jamie was glad and grateful. It was almost as if Pa were still alive. But, of course, he wasn't. I am not so puny as I was then, thought Jamie. I am stronger. I could help Pete close the sluice gate this spring drive. It would not jam, and if Pa fell into the river, I could save him! I'm sure I could save him now.

He thrashed about in his bed, trying to push the rushing water and jumble of logs from his memory. Would it ever leave—that image? Soon it would again be time for the spring drive. The jacks had worked all winter stacking the logs, or sticks as they called them, into pyramids next to the river. When the river was swollen with spring melt, they would release a key log, starting a chain reaction. Mountain upon mountain of logs would plunge into the water; the giant highway of timber twisting and bobbing its way downriver to the sawmills. There were always jams. A log would snag on a boulder giving a hold for others to catch, piling, building, upending, and grinding into a massive jam. It was the river hog's job to single out the stick that had started the whole fiasco, free it then with nimble steps leap from log to log in his death-defying race for shore.

Jamie sat up in bed. A bright moonbeam coming through a lone window spilled across his blanket. The air was chilly but Jamie was damp with sweat. His thoughts were interrupted by a soft clink. He saw his ma's silhouette moving across the moon beam. Jamie was not alone in his sleeplessness.

"Ma?"

"James? Why aren't you asleep?"

"Can't sleep."

"Me neither."

She sat on the end of his bunk. She was wearing a cape over her nightgown.

"Are you going out, Ma?"

"No, son, I was chilly is all. Lie back down."

Jamie slid back under his blanket. Ma touched his forehead.

"You're damp. Are you getting sick?" she said, her voice rising with alarm.

"I feel fine, Ma."

"Are you sure? I'll get you some tea."

She stood.

"I'm fine, Ma, just... had a bad dream, I guess."

She pulled a stool over to Jamie's bedside.

"What was it about?" she asked.

"I'm not sure. Maybe it wasn't a dream. I guess I was just thinkin' about, you know... things."

"About your Pa?"

"Uh huh."

"I think about him too, James." She sighed. "But, it's time to move on with your life. You have a birthday soon. You'll be thirteen. Lordy, how could it be? My boy, almost a man," she muttered wistfully.

"Gray Feather says I'm a man now, according to the Ojibwa."

"Is that how you feel . . . like a man?"

The moonbeam caught her smile across the shadowed face. Jamie thought about Seney and how he had dickered with Smithy at the livery. He also thought about his ma's warm embrace when he and Gray Feather had finally gotten home—that he wanted to get lost in it forever.

"I dunno, sometimes," he finally answered.

The Home Wind

Ma sighed. "James, I was going to discuss something with you. Since neither of us can sleep, I might as well tell you now."

Jamie sat up. Ma had never really discussed anything with him before. She had always told him.

She sighed again and adjusted the folds of her cape on her lap. "After the drive, we will be leaving the logging camp," she began.

Jamie nodded. This was not news. They would have to move into fresh country where the pines stood untouched, ancient, yet innocent as a newborn babe, Pa had once said.

"You and Charlie can ride the wanagan—help feed the men."

Jamie nodded again. The wanagan was a floating dining room designed to feed the rivermen a decent meal during the drive.

"Once the drive is over, we're going to head south. To Manistique." Jamie looked toward his ma. She was staring at her hands.

"Is that the next camp, Manistique?" Jamie asked.

"Well, no, dear. There's a port there, and we're going to catch a steamer."

"A steamer?"

"It's a ship. It will take us west to a place called Menominee. Or rather, we will be going to a sawmill town a few miles from there."

"Is that where camp is going? Is everybody taking the steamer?"

"No, James. I... we won't be cooking for the men anymore."

"But, what then?" An odd feeling was squeezing Jamie.

"Well, first thing I'm going to look for a regular job, make a little more cash. Maybe cooking in a restaurant."

Like Maggie's Eatery! Jamie thought. He remembered the luscious prune whip.

"I'll help, Ma. I'll serve the folks, just like now."

She reached over and touched him. "That's a good boy, James. You have always been such a help. I don't know how I would have done it all these months without your young, strong legs running for me."

But wait. What about Gray Feather? Jamie stiffened. Something squeezed him inside, hard, painful.

"Ma?"

"Yes, son?"

"What about Gray Feather?"

"Charlie?"

"Yes 'um. Will he go too?"

"I'm not sure, dear. They may not let Indians on the steamer. And there's the cost of the fare."

The hand squeezed harder, ever-harder inside him, nearly doubling him over.

"But Ma, he's just got to come! We could disguise him, couldn't we? I get paid this spring, too. We'll have enough money, won't we?"

"Well, James, I don't know. It does complicate things."

"He would help. He could help you in the restaurant, just like now. I know he'd do it for nothing." The hand squeezed the breath from him. His words came between gasps for air.

The Home Wind

Jamie's ma stood and put her hand on his shoulder. "Now calm down, son. You're all worked up. I hadn't thought of Charlie, that's all. I'm sure something can be arranged. If he wants to go, the Lord will help us find a way."

The grip loosened. Jamie took a breath.

"There's one more thing, though, James."

He tensed. Now what?

"It's about Pete. He's going, too."

"Pete?" Jamie said. "He's going to work in the restaurant, too?"

"No, dear. He'll probably get a job in the sawmills. We'll all save our money." Jamie was confused.

"Save for what?"

"We want to buy a little place. Heard there's good farmland at a town called Birch Creek."

"We?"

"We'll be a family… settle down. Get you in a real school, live in a real house."

"You and me—and Gray Feather?"

"Yes, James. You, me—Charlie can fit in somewhere—and then, well, Pete."

"Pete?" Jamie's brain seemed to be stuck into uttering one-word questions.

"Yes, James. Pete and I are to be married."

CHAPTER FOURTEEN
Questions

"I have news of my father," Gray Feather announced matter-of-factly.

Jamie stopped mid bite. He and Gray Feather sat at the tiny table next to the kitchen stove. They were enjoying a repeat experience of prune whip. At least Jamie was. Frothy meringue clung to his upper lip, forming a snowy moustache. His tongue reached up to retrieve every drop.

"What have you heard?" Jamie asked before popping the next bite into his mouth.

His ma was experimenting with new recipes in preparation for looking for a restaurant position. Jamie had mentioned the scrumptious prune whip at Maggie's Eatery. Ma made it for Jamie's thirteenth birthday celebration. It was much tastier than Maggie's.

"I was helping the blacksmith, Bart Hamilton, with some shoeing. He was very excited after returning from a trip. He spoke of two men who were arguing about something—money, he thought."

Jamie finished his dessert and stared at Gray Feather's plate, barely touched.

"Bart went to a blacksmith near Danaher for some steel," Gray Feather continued. "He told me of a very rude man that he met. The man was arguing with the smithy.

The Home Wind

He—the rude man—was getting ready to punch the smithy, until Bart stepped in."

"So, what's that got to do with your father?" Jamie licked his lips and pointed at Gray Feather's plate. "You gonna eat that?"

Gray Feather shoved his plate toward Jamie. "Happy birthday, my friend. Don't get a stomachache."

Once again Jamie could feel a foamy mustache clinging to his lip.

"Bart told me that the smithy in Germfask shouted the name of this rude man, Angus MacGregor, and what a queer name he thought that was. Scottish he supposed."

"But maybe it's not the right Angus MacGregor." Jamie was getting full. He contemplated the last bite on his plate, shrugged, and scooped it up with his spoon.

"It is him. There cannot be many Angus MacGregors in these parts. Bart described him, too: red hair, red moustache and a scar on his cheek. Yes, James, it was my Angus MacGregor."

Jamie felt like a stuffed goose. Lunch barely digested then two helpings of dessert. He reached to his waist and touched the handle of his new knife. It was a beautiful knife given to him by Pete, Gray Feather and Ma. Pete had honed the blade and Gray Feather had carved the handle from a deer antler. Ma had sewn the sheath that attached to his belt. She was not entirely enthusiastic about the gift, but evidently Pete had pointed out that Jamie was doing a man's work and should be allowed to carry a knife.

"Bart also found out where Angus MacGregor is heading," Gray Feather continued.

Jamie's hand gripped the knife handle. It could only mean one thing. Gray Feather would be following his father—to Timbuktu, if necessary. Jamie felt the prune whip churn in his stomach.

"Where—where's he headed?"

"Well, my friend, it seems Angus MacGregor is also heading to Manistique to catch the steamer to Menominee."

"But we're not leaving for a while, Gray Feather. We'll miss him," Jamie said.

"That is true. He will leave before us, but our destination is the same. Perhaps he will get work in the same sawmills that Pete speaks of. I will catch him, James. I am getting closer." Gray Feather's eyes gleamed hard and dark.

In spite of his relief that Gray Feather would be traveling with them to Menominee, Jamie's belly still felt unsettled. Why couldn't he give up this crazy notion of vengeance? Jamie would do anything, go anywhere, if only his father were alive. He would even be willing to live in the tiny wilderness cabin. His ma and Pete would be getting married soon. Having Pete for a pa would be okay, Jamie supposed, but he would never be his real father.

Tom Haskins stuck his head through the cook house doorway. "Teamsters are back," he barked. "Get out there and unharness the horses."

Jamie saw Gray Feather stiffen at the sight of the boss man. Why did Tom Haskins despise the Indian? Gray Feather had done nothing but work hard for only food and a pallet in the stable. Jamie sighed, his bloated stomach protesting his gluttony.

The Home Wind

"Best go work off some of this grub," Jamie said, rising from his chair. Gray Feather remained sitting, staring at the doorway where Tom Haskins had been.

Ma walked in and began feeding firewood into the stove. She was humming again. Jamie guessed he should be glad. He knew it was her betrothal to Pete that was making her so perky.

"You boys get enough dessert?" she chirped.

"I did, Ma," Jamie said.

She eyed the two plates in front of Jamie.

"Why Charlie, didn't you like it? You're feeling all right, aren't you?"

"I am fine, Mrs. Kangas. Just not hungry. The food is always good," Gray Feather said.

He stood and managed to smile.

The boys went outside as the teams of horses were being driven into the camp clearing.

The days had gradually become warmer, so the roads could no longer be iced for pulling the sleds. Instead, the horses were hitched to giant wheels so enormous that Jamie's head barely reached the hub. This was so they could clear the ever-growing number of tree stumps. Cut to size, the gigantic logs were heaved into chain slings that hung from the contraption, then hauled to the river. The Fox River was rising as the melting snow rushed along rivulets and ditches to its banks. The seemingly endless forests of white pine were being replaced by countless pyramids of logs stacked along the riverbanks. Jamie was glad that this spring drive required no dams or sluice gates, the water being high and fast enough to carry the glut of timber downriver to the sawmills.

Jamie and Gray Feather unharnessed the horses and took them to the stable. Soon the spring drive would arrive and the horses would be sent off to the next camp where more rustic buildings would be erected. Come fall, it would start all over.

But not for Jamie. And not for Gray Feather or Ma or Pete. Jamie was not sorrowed by this change of events. Nothing could be so difficult as the life of a chore boy. And Ma was happy. Jamie had not thought much before of her happiness. He had been too preoccupied with his own grief to think of hers. He was stabbed with pangs of guilt for his selfishness.

Once the teams of horses had been unharnessed, it was time to help with supper. No, Jamie would not miss the dashing back and forth from kitchen to mess hall. Waiting on more civilized folks in a restaurant, as Ma had said, would be an improvement. And then they would build a little place of their own and put down some roots, she said. They would plant crops, raise some chickens, and maybe there would be a brother or sister for Jamie. That thought made him bristle. Jamie envisioned a squalling infant being thrust into his arms for safekeeping then, when it got older, clinging to him like a burr, whining for this or that. Gray Feather was like a brother to Jamie, he needed no other siblings. One thing was certain, nobody asked Jamie. If a baby brother or sister were to come, then Jamie guessed there wasn't much he could do to stop it.

Jamie sat alone next to the kitchen stove waiting for the dishwater to heat. Ma had gone for a walk with Pete. Jamie pulled his knife out of the sheath. The blade glinted as he turned it. A knife has many uses, Pete had told him. Of course, you can skin and dress out your game. It's good for hacking off small branches when an axe isn't handy. It'll do for snake bite or a game of mumbly peg. But sometimes the best thing a knife can do is whittle. Jamie expected this meant carving a stick to a sharp point or cutting the bark off a branch before rubbing it smooth.

But it was Gray Feather who had told him otherwise.

"You take a piece of wood and study it. Everything has a spirit within it: the rocks, the trees, even a piece of wood. If you look long enough, you will find it: the image of an animal, a vision of the future. Once you see it, you must carefully remove the pieces that don't belong. When you are done, you will find the life of the wood."

Jamie picked up a piece of kindling from the wood pile next to the stove. He turned it over and over, looking for the mysterious shape that was supposed to jump out at him. Try as he did, all he could see was a stick. He picked through the woodpile, searching for a more inspirational piece of wood, stuffing each rejected piece through the top of the stove into the fire. As the fire grew, the kitchen became uncomfortably warm and sweat trickled down Jamie's brow.

You cannot force it to reveal itself, Gray Feather had told him. It is like waiting for a deer, you must be patient.

Jamie had never been patient. With unsettled desperation, he rifled through the pile of firewood, determined to find the right piece of wood to set his new blade to. He was certain if he could find that certain piece, it would end the gnawing feeling inside him, answer the questions that raced through his head. What would it be like, moving to Menominee with Ma and Pete?

What if they couldn't find work?

"And what about Gray Feather?" Jamie asked a gnarly piece of kindling. Would he be sent off to jail if he killed his father? Jamie was afraid for his friend and for himself. What would he do without Gray Feather at his side, teaching him, protecting him?

A dozen more pieces of wood met their fiery end. The water was sending plumes of steam into the sweltering kitchen. Jamie put the knife back into its sheath and rolled up his sleeves. Using a towel on the handle, he lifted the kettle of water off the stove and poured some into the waiting dish pan. He rolled up his sleeves and scraped shavings from a bar of soap into the water. The dirty dishes towered around him. He stared into the suds then dropped a stack of plates into them. The soap foam undulated into many shapes, taunting him with more mystery. Surely there was more than soap suds in his future; more than raising chickens and tending a snot-nosed brother or sister.

Jamie glanced at the woodpile. Maybe it was too angry to give up its secrets to a lumber camp chore boy. Jamie had fed the men who, with unrelenting determination, had cut acre after acre of trees. He had harnessed the horses that had hauled the fallen trees to the river. Though Jamie had never wielded an axe or crosscut saw, he had been a part. A chill ran through him, making him shiver in spite of the stifling heat of the kitchen.

Jamie dropped the scrubbed plates into the scalding tub of rinse water, scorching his hands. Jamie didn't care if he ever saw another dirty dish. He hoped someone else would do the dishes when Ma got a job in a restaurant and Jamie could help cook or wait on the customers.

Maybe he could make it right, the destruction of the forests. Maybe if he did, the spirit of his father would rest. But how? Even if he knew what to do, who would listen to a boy? Gingerly, Jamie reached for the plates in the rinse water.

Once his father had shown him the beginning of a tree rising from the forest floor.

It all starts with a pinecone, son, Pa had said. If it's lucky, it'll fall into a patch of ground warmed by the sun. A little rain and warmth, and the cone will sprout, like a kernel of corn, and a tiny piece of green will push from the earth. Eventually, a miniature tree trunk will form, no bigger than a flower stem, and needles will spring out, reaching for a little sunshine. Next come the branches. Under the soil, the roots spread, looking for moisture and nutrients.

Jamie put the clean plates on the shelves and turned his attention to the cups, knives, and forks. The water was starting to cool but his hands were still an angry red.

A lot can happen to this little tree, his pa had explained. The older ones may block the sunlight and steal the water from the soil, starving it. A browsing deer may eat it or trample it. But with each passing year, it grows a little stronger and the odds are a little better for survival. As the decades pass, it reaches for the sun, stretching tall and straight into the sky. Now it can fall victim to the whims of the wind or storms. A bolt of lightning may come from the sky, splitting it open, boiling its sap, leaving it to wither and die. Then there are fires, sweeping across the land, devouring the trees like matchsticks.

Jamie finished with the cutlery and coffee cups. He wiped his wrinkled hands on a towel then carried the dishwater out the cook house door, slopping a little on his shirt as he went. He tossed the water into a small patch of snow, melting it away. The rinse water would be saved; reheated for the next meal's dishwater. Jamie stared at the diminishing patch of grainy snow. There was more mud than snow, now, especially where the horses' sharp hooves had churned up the earth.

Jamie looked at a giant white pine on the rim of the lumber camp.

Takes hundreds of years, boy, to get that big, Pa had said. When it was born, white man had not yet come to these parts.

A sudden breeze floated from the pine boughs with a hush. It feathered Jamie's hair and cascaded down his neck, his arms, to his fingertips. It was surprisingly warm, almost caressing.

"Pa?"

But the pine boughs stilled and the breeze was gone. All that remained were Jamie's unanswered questions.

PART TWO

MENOMINEE RIVER MILL TOWN

CHAPTER FIFTEEN
Riding the Waves

The steamer, *George L. Dunlap*, heaved over another wave, making Jamie wish he had skipped breakfast. Gray Feather had long since lost his over the railing. It alarmed Jamie to see his friend in such a state. Gray Feather's normal bronze coloring was splotched and pasty. He clung to the railing along the deck, horror washing over his face as the steamer pitched and bucked through the rough waters of Lake Michigan. Jamie could do little to comfort him, barely able to contain his own growing panic. Vicious waves lashed the boat hull often sending a spray of foam over the railing onto the deck where the boys shivered in cold, wet terror.

Ma and Pete were warm and safe in their passenger compartment. For reasons unknown to Jamie, they had sent the boys to "get some fresh air" for an hour or so. Jamie was just as glad to leave the cramped cabin where the rolling of the ship left his stomach unsettled. His ma had fed the boys hunks of bread slathered with lard before boarding the ship. Jamie suspected it was the lard that churned inside him. He and Gray Feather had briefly explored the steamer, inspecting its cargo of lumber destined for Chicago. Next, they went to the ship's rustic parlor where passengers sat in chairs bolted to the deck, reading books or nibbling food. Gray Feather drew hostile stares from some of the passengers and soon the boys took refuge on the deck. Gray Feather had grown quiet and withdrawn and suddenly raced to the railing where, leaning over the side, he heaved into the angry water below.

A crew hand approached and laughed at the boys.

"Indian looks like he's seen a ghost," the sailor snickered.

The bow of the ship rose and slapped down into a trough, sending another spray of foam onto the shivering boys.

"We picked up a fresh breeze is all, lads. Once we get around the point and into De Noc, she'll be calm as a kitten."

"Soon, I hope, or I may use my knife to end it all." Gray Feather moved from the railing and leaned against the wall of the pilot house. He slid down the wall, slow and thick like molasses on the side of a barrel. He didn't seem to notice he was sitting in a puddle of water. He shivered, yet sweat beaded his forehead.

The sailor laughed again. He stood, legs splayed, his torso seeming unaffected by the movement of the boat. He pulled a piece of sausage from his pocket and took a large, greasy bite.

"Wanna try some?" he asked, thrusting the oily meat into Gray Feather's face.

The laughter soon turned to shouts of outrage when Gray Feather vomited on the sailor's boots.

"Damn you Indian! The captain'll have me hide!" The sailor drew his hand back to strike Gray Feather who gazed blankly at his adversary.

"No," Jamie cried. He jumped between the sailor and Gray Feather and turned his shoulder to the blow. The sailor's hand caught Jamie in the elbow causing the sailor to yelp in pain.

"Serves you right," Jamie snorted. The sailor stomped around the deck seeking relief for the injured hand by shaking it. Jamie's elbow tingled, nearly paralyzed, but he'd have eaten the sausage before he'd let on.

Gray Feather staggered to his feet, gamely trying to ready himself for the battle that was sure to follow.

"Why you brats, I think you broke me hand," howled the sailor, pressing his hand into his armpit.

"What're doing, picking on a couple'a boys?"

Jamie whirled around to see Pete standing on the deck, throwing a hard look at the sailor.

"I was just having a little sport with th' lads. If me hand's broke, I'll not be able to unload at the docks," the sailor whined.

"Doesn't look broke to me," Pete said. "But your boots could use a spit shine."

The sailor glared at Pete. "If it weren't for me hand, I'd take you on. I've thrashed a fair number of men in my day."

"I'd venture that it's only young 'uns and maybe womenfolk that you'd choose to knock about," said Pete, fists clenched at his sides. "I know your kind. Where I come from we don't call it sport, we call it cowardice."

The sailor's jaw tightened, rheumy eyes blinking.

The steam whistle blew, startling everyone. Gray Feather collapsed and slid back down the wall into a limp heap on the deck. Jamie crouched next to him, dabbing his friend's forehead with his bandana.

"That's me captain calling. You're off the hook this time," snarled the sailor as he stalked off.

The Home Wind

"I think Ma should take a look at Gray Feather," Jamie said.

Pete knelt next to Gray Feather. "The boat ride sure has knocked the stuffing out of Charlie. Gimme a hand, James, we'll get him to the cabin."

Jamie grunted as he and Pete laid Gray Feather on the sole bed in the cabin. Ma had quickly smoothed the blanket and plumped the pillow. Jamie glanced at her. Her hair, normally in a tight bun, cascaded around her shoulders and her blouse ballooned loosely out of the back of her skirt, as if she had made a hasty attempt to tuck it in. She wore no stockings or shoes, scurrying barefoot across the rough planks of the cabin. Ma opened the window of the cabin allowing an icy wind to cut into the stuffy warmth. She dipped a towel into a bucket of water which hung from a hook on the wall. Kneeling next to Gray Feather, she dabbed the residue of vomit from his mouth.

"We need some fresh drinking water for Charlie and an empty bucket in case he has anything left to come up," Ma said.

Jamie scurried out of the cabin, fetching fresh water and an extra bucket from the passenger parlor.

Ma heated tea on the tiny cabin stove. Gray Feather sipped tentatively, grasping the cup with trembling hands. Jamie felt his stomach rumble, not with nausea, but rather hunger. He didn't dare suggest they have lunch for fear it would send his friend into another spell of retching. Jamie felt the coins in his pocket. Maybe there would be food to buy in the passenger parlor.

"Okay if I go for a walk, Ma?"

"Certainly, James, but please be careful."

Jamie glanced at Pete and they exchanged a look.

"Stay where folks are," Pete said.

Jamie nodded. His ma was too busy with Gray Feather to notice Pete's concern. Back on deck, Jamie was pleased to notice that the waves had lessened causing the *Dunlap* to rock like a cradle rather than pitch like a demon. Sunshine poked through the haze, drying his damp clothing and warming his chilled bones. He found he way into the parlor and found a crew man selling fresh cornbread and coffee. Jamie bought a slab of cornbread, his mouth watering as he watched the man douse it with blackstrap molasses. Jamie settled himself into a chair and bit into his cornbread. He licked the molasses from his fingers and lips, savoring its bitter sweetness. The cornbread quickly disappeared and Jamie washed it down with a cup of strong, hot coffee. He wished that Gray Feather could enjoy the treat. He wondered if he should bring him back a piece, but remembering his friend's reaction to the sausage, thought better.

The steam whistle blew again, making Jamie jump and spill his coffee. He shrugged looking at the new stain on his pants which blended with the old. There had been no time for laundry after the long trip from Seney to Manistique where they had caught the steamer. After Ma and Pete's simple marriage ceremony in the little whitewashed church in Seney, the four of them had ridden their horses hard for two days to catch the *Dunlap* that was picking up a load of lumber from the mills for shipment to Illinois. The steamer took on passengers at Manistique who were traveling to Escanaba, Menominee, and as far south

as Chicago, Illinois. He had been told that they would reach
Escanaba before dark where they would take on firewood
and exchange passengers. They would dock there for the
night. The next day would find them at their final destination: Menominee, where they would try to catch a ride to
the sawmill town several miles away. The venture was
filled with uncertainties. Pete would look for work in the
sawmills and Ma in a restaurant. But what if none were to
be found? Would they be paupers, reduced to begging in
the street like the thin, ragged Indians Jamie had seen at
Manistique?

The steam whistle blew again. Jamie was becoming accustomed to it and he barely flinched. He rose from his
chair and went on deck along with many of the passengers.
Land had been out of sight for some time while they
crossed the foggy stretch of open water from Pt. DeTour to
Escanaba. He stared at the horizon straining to see what
the others were pointing at. Eventually he could see the
outline of land which lay on the horizon. A sharp wind
again picked up, sending many of the passengers back into
the shelter of the boat. Jamie stayed on deck waiting for
the silhouette of land to grow closer. But it seemed to elude
the *Dunlap*, remaining a greenish hump in the distance.
Thick clouds scudded through the sky, obliterating the brief
interlude of sunshine. Mist rose as if the water were on fire.

Jeebi was what Gray Feather called the early-morning
mists that shrouded the shores of lakes and islands. The
Jeebi is a ghost, a spirt that floats free while searching
for its soul. Jamie stared at the halo of fog that clung to
the distant landscape. He felt vaguely akin to it. Maybe

when they reached their final destination, the fog would settle. Ma had told him they must move on with their lives—that the grieving time for Pa was over. True to her words, she had married Pete. Gray Feather had talked about Jamie ridding himself of the *Mitchi Manitou* that gnawed at him. But how, Jamie wondered as he watched the distant land grow nearer. When, he asked himself, will the fog melt away?

Even with the first drops of rain, Jamie remained steadfast at the railing, waiting for evidence of the boat's progress. The rain grew heavier and Jamie turned up his coat collar.

At last the distant knoll grew, like a giant serpent rising from the choppy water. With grinding determination, the Dunbar labored toward the harbor. The boat's whistle blared nonstop and smoke belched from its stack.

The rain pummeled Jamie, forcing him to retreat to the cabin. When he entered, he found Gray Feather sitting on the bunk. A blotch of color had returned to his cheeks. Pete was absently rubbing a rag across the dried mud on his boots and Ma was tidying the cabin.

"Oh good, James, you're back. We should all have something to eat. Biscuits and salt pork will have to do," Ma said as she dug into a rucksack.

"I had some cornbread," Jamie said.

His ma paused, her hand buried in the depths of the rucksack. "You bought food?" she asked.

"Um, well, I was hungry and I . . ." Suddenly the cornbread became a lump inside him.

"James, you know we can't indulge in such luxuries!" she scolded.

The Home Wind

All eyes were on him, as if he had just confessed to devil worship.

"I...I'm sorry, Ma. I guess I didn't think. It wasn't but a few cents."

His ma sighed and turned her attention back to the bag. She produced some stale biscuits wrapped in a cloth. She passed around the biscuits, skipping Jamie. The whistle blew again, three consecutive blasts.

"We'll be docking soon," Pete said, chewing his dried-out biscuit. He glanced at the biscuit, then at Jamie and gave him a wink. "We'll have to take some meals as they come, Anja," Pete said.

Jamie's heart lightened. At least Pete was not angry with him. He had not thought he was being selfish. He had thought about bringing cornbread back for the others, but was afraid he would make Gray Feather sicker. Jamie watched Gray Feather chew unenthusiastically.

"Yes, I suppose so," Ma said. "But, James, we have to watch every nickel. Just because you have money in your pocket doesn't mean you have to spend it."

Jamie lowered his chin to his chest. "Yes Ma'am," he muttered. After all, Jamie thought, it's money I earned. What was the use of having it if you couldn't decide what to spend it on?

Pete stood and brushed the crumbs off his hands. "Your ma's right, James. We've got to make our money last. But it won't cost anything to get off the infernal boat for a few hours and go into town. We won't be sailing again until daybreak."

"That's a wonderful idea, dear," Ma said. "Charlie, do you feel up to it?"

"Yes, Mrs. Kangas—er, Mrs. Atkins. I would very much enjoy getting off this demon canoe," Gray Feather said with a weak smile.

Pete laughed and laid his hand on Gray Feather's shoulder. "We've got a ways to go again tomorrow, Charlie, but then we'll be, well, home!"

Ma stood and fussed with the combs in her hair. "Won't it be grand! James, smooth your hair and, oh my Lord, look at you. What I wouldn't do for a laundry tub and line. Well, never mind. It'll just have to wait. We look like a bunch of emigrants."

But she was laughing and the cornbread transgression was forgotten. Yes, it was all very grand.

CHAPTER SIXTEEN
Number 47

The little salt-box house stood in sad neglect at the edge of a muddy, nameless street. Its weathered siding had never seen even a coat of whitewash and the listing porch bounced with each footstep. Inside, grime coated the floors and rude pieces of furniture. A much smaller version of the lumber camp cast-iron stove squatted in a corner, the wall behind it alarmingly charred. Yellowing sheets of newspaper hung limply from the walls. There was an extra room separated from the main room by a wall with a lopsided door cut into it. At one time, a burlap curtain had probably hung over the doorway, but now only a few shreds of unraveled cloth remained.

No one spoke at first as they surveyed their derelict surroundings. Gray sunlight cast a weak beam through the grime-caked windows.

"Look, boys," Pete said, "your own sleeping loft!"

Jamie and Gray Feather shifted their attention to a steep, rickety stairway rising to the loft Jamie squinted through the generously spaced gaps between the loft floor planking. Some of the boards looked rotten. Jamie suspected that was from rainwater and snow coming through the hole in the roof.

Jamie's ma sighed. "Well, this isn't fit for even a mountain man to live in."

The Home Wind

"It's a roof over our heads—more or less," Pete said, scowling at the hole in the roof. "First thing is to get that roof patched, then these steps."

"First thing is to get this dirt swept out of here! And knock down these cobwebs." Ma put her hands on her hips and turned to look out a window. "And scrub these filthy windows. I suspect we could see the river from here, but I can't tell for all the dirt."

Jamie was bone weary. So were the rest, he figured. After docking, they had spent another night aboard the ship, waiting for early light to begin their new venture. With rubbery legs, they had stumbled off the boat, claimed their trunks, and had given a man two bits to haul them and their belongings to the sawmill. Pete had heard that the company would hire any able- bodied man on the spot. Crammed in the back of the wagon, they bounced and bumped their way through the mill town, past rows of ramshackle houses and other buildings that housed the blacksmith, the company store—like Baumgartner's in Seney—a church, school, doctor's house, and of course the large, rambling sawmill.

Founded out of necessity, the Menominee River sawmill town held little charm or beauty. It was hacked out of the wilderness, much like a logging camp, with little thought given to design. Tree stumps littered the town, which was built on low-lying land in order to be near the river. Water from rain and snow melt found its way down the eroded hills into the little town, turning the streets into mud and flooding the houses and barns of folks unfortunate enough to live on the lowest parts.

The driver pointed to an opulent house perched on top of a hill. The sawmill owner and his wife lived there, he explained. They were called the baron and baroness. To Jamie, the house looked as out of place as a top hat on a mule.

"Payday's once a month, after expenses are taken out," the foreman had growled. "You plannin' on the boy working?" he asked, glaring down his bulbous nose at Jamie. "Looks kind of puny."

Jamie's ma put a protective arm around his shoulders. "No, my son will be finding a job in a restaurant with me." Jamie felt a flush creep up his neck.

The man shrugged. "Good luck, Missus, we've got no restaurant, 'less you want to go all the way back to Menominee, seven miles yonder."

"Oh, dear," she said, turning to look at Pete.

"Don't worry, there's plenty of work for a woman here," the foreman said. "Company store always needs a clerk. Boy can stock shelves. Maybe help him grow some muscle." Jamie felt his face go hot as the foreman sneered at him.

"Indian can work in the mill," the foreman said, "but at half pay. You be needin' a house?"

"Yes," Ma said, "something decent."

"Uh huh." The foreman flipped through the pages of a ledger until he found a blank one.

He wrote something at the top.

"You'll be in number forty-seven," the foreman had barked. "Last house on the street heading south out of town," he added, jerking a thumb over his shoulder. "Needs some work."

The Home Wind

Exhausted, they had trudged down the muddy street to house number 47, ready to collapse and get some rest. Instead of rest, however, the four were faced with the filthy, ramshackle little house. It seemed impossible to know what to do first. Clean? Repair? Jamie felt an urge to get back on the boat and sail far, far away.

Ma drew her frame up straight. "James, see if there's a broom anywhere. Charlie, fetch some water from the well. I pray to the Lord that we have a clean well and some buckets. Otherwise, we'll have to go to the mercantile and start a tally sheet."

Pete continued to stare at the hole in the roof. "I reckon we'll have to go to the store, regardless, for some lumber, shingles, and nails. And a ladder."

Ma sighed. "We haven't been here but a few hours and already we have to go into debt."

A kerosene lantern had been added to the growing list of goods bought on credit and, later that night, it was by its dim light that Jamie and Gray Feather dragged themselves up the hastily repaired ladder to the crude sleeping loft. It was swept clean, now, and the roof patched. The boys fell on top of a blanket which would serve as a sleeping pallet until a mattress could be made. They had found a washtub behind the privy and tomorrow Jamie and his ma would launder clothes while Pete and Gray Feather reported for their first day at the mill.

Waves of disappointment washed over Jamie. He wanted to be with Pete and Gray Feather at the mill, running the screaming saws, watching them bite through the massive logs. He was mortified to be assigned to women's work, scrubbing the family laundry. Then they were to get provisions for the larder and do more cleaning. Jamie lay awake, enraged at the prospect of such unmanly tasks. Why was Ma so protective of him? No, James, stay away from that ladder, she had shrieked when he wanted to help Pete with the roof. How would he ever grow muscular, like his pa, if she had him washing dishes and chopping potatoes? If she had her way, she would probably tie an apron around his waist.

Jamie tossed and turned on the hard, splintered floor. Gray Feather snored softly beside him. He could fall asleep anywhere. Jamie had become accustomed to having a mattress. He supposed that maybe he was soft. His thoughts drifted once again to their new life in the sawmill town. When the household was in order, Jamie and his ma would visit the mercantile and inquire about a job. Jamie prayed he would be assigned to stocking merchandise and helping ladies with their heavy bundles. Maybe he would build some muscles.

Here, Ma, let me move that stove for you! He smiled in the darkness. Why, James, you've become so strong! She would twitter. Now you scoot on outside and help Pete put that new roof on the barn. That was more like it. Not, James, mind you keep your clothes clean. Or, James, be careful you don't hurt yourself carrying that firewood!

Jamie felt sleep overtake him and his thoughts turned to dreams. Dreams of bulging arms bursting the seams on his shirt. He dreamed of plucking huge logs from the river jam and tossing them like matchsticks downriver. With barely a tap of his fist the sluice gate would slide into place.

The Home Wind

Jamie saw the lines of exhaustion on Pete's face. It was hard work, Jamie imagined, but surely it was better than having prune-wrinkled hands rubbed raw on a washboard. Gray Feather had not been allowed near the saws, but instead spent his day by the river helping the scaler tally the logs.

"I had to learn the different marks that each logging company brands onto the end of their logs. Then I called them out to the scaler and he kept a count," Gray Feather said.

Jamie had spent the day scrubbing laundry, bending over a washboard and tub until his back screamed in pain and his hands were cracked and sore from the harsh bar of soap and scalding water. He and Ma had wrung out the clothes, each taking an end, then twisting and twisting.

"Sometimes, log thieves will cut off the end of a log, removing the brand, then mark it with their own brand," Gray Feather continued.

Jamie and his ma had hung the heavy, soggy clothes on the line, Jamie straining to reach, his arms and shoulders aching with the effort. Jealousy crept into him like the cold finding its way to his bones. Why was an Indian allowed to have such a wonderful job, while Jamie was left behind to do such demeaning tasks as the family laundry? It still hung on the line he and Ma had strung between two trees. Then Jamie felt shame for being angry with his friend. Why shouldn't Gray Feather have the job helping the scaler? Being an Indian had nothing to do with it, he told himself. It shouldn't matter. Was he starting to think like other people—Tom Haskins, the shopkeeper in Seney, the livery stable owner—that an Indian was somehow… less than a person? Jamie was alarmed at the prospect. He would never be like them. Never!

"If you're done with your supper, James, please go pull the clothes off the line," Ma said. "I'm sure Pete and Charlie are very tired after their first day at work. After you get the laundry, you and I will clean up the dishes and they can relax. Later, Charlie can read us a verse from the Bible."

Jamie clenched his jaw so tight he felt it pop. Pete glanced at him. "Anything wrong, James?" Jamie swallowed hard and shook his head. Pete watched his wife pick up the dirty dishes and put them in the washtub.

"Hurry up, James. The laundry—now!"

Jamie sat as if glued to his seat, fists clenched at his sides. Pete stood, grabbing a handful of dishes and carried them to the washtub.

"Ah, Anja, I think we should all help. I'm sure you and James are every bit as done in as Charlie and me. Better yet, why don't you and I do these dishes, and, uh, Charlie and James can get the things off the line."

Jamie's ma gave her husband a strange look. Jamie relaxed his fists, tension easing.

"Why, Peter Atkins, since when does a man do lowly woman's work?" she said, taking the dishes from him and putting them in the tub.

Pete jerked his head toward Jamie and rolled his eyes. Ma looked at him as if he were possessed. "Whatever is wrong with you?" she said. "Now don't you touch another plate. I told you, James and I will handle the chores."

Jamie bolted from his chair, tipping it over with a clatter. "I'm a man, too!" he screamed, pounding his fists on the table. "I don't want to do any more dishes! Do you hear me, Ma? I will run away and hide in the woods and eat raw meat with my bare hands if I have to, but I don't want to wash any more dishes, or do any laundry, or cook, or work in a nice, safe store with you in town, I…" he faltered, his ma's shocked eyes on him.

"James!"

"Well, I don't, Ma. I want to go to the sawmill with Pete and Gray Feather!" Suddenly, Jamie's rage was spent and he felt very tired. Pete, Gray Feather, and Ma stared at him, their mouths agape.

Jamie raced from the room and banged the door open. He stormed down the steps into the yard and stared at the clean laundry flapping in the breeze. He wanted to yank it off the line, drag it through the mud and stuff it down the privy. That's what he wanted to do. But she would just make him re-wash it, and that would surely drive him completely mad. He would foam at the mouth like a rabid fox and run through the muddy streets until captured and thrown into a dank prison to rot for all eternity. Still, it would feel good for a short while, mashing the clothes into the mud then watching them drop into the repulsive pit of the outhouse.

He felt his ma's hand on his shoulder. He turned to look at her.

"I'll get this off the line, James. You go rest with the other . . . men."

Her face was drawn with worry and fatigue. When had her hair turned so gray? Shame slapped him like a winter wind. How could he be so selfish?

"No, Ma," he said. "I'll get this and you go rest."

Their eyes locked for a moment. Hers looked so tired and faded. He watched them fill with tears.

"Oh, James," she said, her voice quaking, "what would I ever do without you?"

CHAPTER SEVENTEEN
A Race To The River

"One hundred and thirty-two dollars," Ma announced with a satisfaction. Greenbacks, silver dollars and a few other coins lay on the table in neat stacks.

Pete sat down at the table and inspected the family savings that his wife had pulled from storage in its tea tin.

"Is it enough?" she asked.

"I think so, Anja. I hear you can purchase a farm at Birch Creek for a hundred dollars. I'd like more extra than we got. It didn't build up like I had hoped. The cost of things is a lot higher than I'd planned. Five dollars a month for this house!"

"They should pay us to live here," Jamie said. "It wouldn't be worth two dollars a month if we hadn't fixed it up."

"Then there's the other things," Ma said. "Food, cloth for sewing, so many things just to live. I never thought about having to buy so much. At the lumber camp, we just went to the foreman and asked for goods and, of course, the meals were all provided."

Gray Feather came through the door from outside, carrying a basket. It looked empty to Jamie. "I am afraid the chickens have stopped laying eggs, Mrs. Atkins."

Ma sighed then carefully put the family savings back into its storage tin. "It's the drought. The garden never did much. I was afraid to use water from the well because it was drying up."

The Home Wind

"We could have hauled more from the river, Ma," Jamie said.

"I know, James, but it's nearly a quarter of a mile. It's all we can do to have enough for cooking and washing. You'd have spent all day hauling buckets to water the garden and I needed you at the store."

Pete wiped his brow with the back of his hand. "Hard to believe it's October. This is the hottest Indian summer I remember. I don't think we had a drop of rain all August or September."

"Well, enough of this dreary talk," Ma said. "I'm sure it will rain soon, I can feel it in the air. Now let's all go to church and pray for it."

Jamie tugged at the collar of his good shirt. It was getting tight. They left the house and began the short walk to church. Jamie shuffled through the dusty street. He felt sticky and gritty all over. When they had arrived at the mill town in the spring, the streets had been thick with mud, bogging wagons and caking on the hem of Ma's skirt. Now plumes of dust rose with each footstep and a team of horses would churn up a cloud thick enough to choke a man. Wells were drying up and cows had quit giving milk. Tinder-dry brush littered the denuded landscape as far as the eye could see. A fire had broken out at the sawmill, ignited by a spark from the big saw. A disorganized brigade of men had scurried around getting buckets of water to put it out, but not before it spread to a dried-up peat bog, which still smoldered in the distance, sending an occasional whiff of smoke into town. There was talk of the company buying a fire wagon specially made to hold water used to put out fires. Pete had said that the owner thought it was a waste of money being that the river was right next to the mill.

Jamie settled uncomfortably onto the hard bench inside the stifling church. He sat in the back with Gray Feather, while Pete and Ma took a seat closer to front. Many of the ladies were fanning themselves and men wiped their brows with handkerchiefs. Jamie had neither a fan nor a handkerchief and squirmed miserably while rivulets of sweat ran down his back into the waist of his trousers. Except for a few beads of sweat on his brow, Gray Feather seem unaffected by the heat.

Suddenly, everyone was standing and bleating out the strains of a hymn that Jamie did not know. He moved his lips half-heartedly. He wondered if Ma would let Gray Feather and him go to the river for a swim. Water was too precious for a real bath and, as much as he hated to admit it, he longed to be clean. Jamie glanced over at Gray Feather who stood straight and stoic, enduring the Christian ritual of hymn singing. Their eyes locked for a moment. Jamie had seen the haunted look before in his friend. Something was happening with Gray Feather. What was it?

Everyone was sitting again. Jamie and Gray Feather quickly took their seats. Jamie leaned over to Gray Feather and whispered to him. "What's the matter, Gray Feather? Something's the matter, I can tell."

Gray Feather opened his mouth to speak just as the preacher, red faced and sweating, began his sermon. Gray Feather shook his head and whispered back, "Later."

Jamie sighed and wished the preaching would get over with. Jamie could feel the perspiration pooling in his new shoes. Ma had bought them when Jamie could no longer force his growing feet into his old ones. He would be drenched from head to toe by the time they escaped the infernally hot church. Jamie was beginning to think that this must be what hell was like. He didn't think much of it and vowed to be a better Christian, just in case he was headed in the wrong direction. Best start by paying attention to the preacher.

Folks were standing again. He knew a few of the words to this hymn. His ma had sung it to him often but usually he had just listened to the lilt of her voice, soothing and re-assuring, rather than the words.

Gray Feather leaned toward Jamie. "I saw Angus MacGregor yesterday. He has been in Menominee all summer, I am told. Now he has arrived at the mill to settle up for his company, Thomkins-Watson. I did not recognize him at first."

Jamie's mouth froze mid-note. "Your father?" he whispered.

Gray Feather nodded.

The hymn ended and everyone sat down. The collection basket was being brought down the aisle and passed along the rows. Jamie felt in his pocket for a penny.

"I know these are difficult times," bleated the preacher, "but dig deep, my friends. We have many widows and orphans who must rely on your generosity. Of special mention is the Johnston family. I'm sure you have all heard of the accident."

"Ben almost had his arm cut clean off," muttered a man next to Jamie. "Blasted saw should have a guard."

Jamie plunked his penny into the basket. It was all he had. His mind raced with the image of Mr. Johnston's arm hanging by a few scraps of skin. He shuddered.

Jamie leaned toward Gray Feather and whispered, "Did he see you—your father?"

"It is possible, but he does not recognize me, I am sure."

"What are you going to do?"

"I will wait."

"Wait?"

"The spirits will guide me."

"You gonna kill him?"

"I will know at the time."

Why did Gray Feather speak in such riddles? Jamie felt desperate to know what his friend intended to do. If Gray Feather killed a white man, they would lock him up, maybe even kill him too. Jamie wished he could stop Gray Feather, but how?

"Maybe it wasn't him. You want to make sure, don't you?" Jamie said.

"It was him. He wore the scar on his cheek, though he tries to disguise it with a beard. But the hair has not grown well over the scar. Yes, I am certain it was Angus MacGregor who I saw."

Everybody was standing and shuffling out of the church. The preacher stood at the door, offering a damp hand to the members of his congregation.

Jamie caught fragments of conversation. "Hope we get rain soon...fires south of here...goin' back to Ohio before winter."

The Home Wind

"God Bless you son," said the preacher shaking Jamie's hand. Gray Feather did not offer his, but the preacher did not seem to notice.

"Thank you, Reverend," Jamie muttered, absently wiping his hand on his trousers.

"Do you know where he's staying—your father?" Jamie asked.

"No. But I am sure he will stay in town until his lumber is milled and he settles up for his outfit. They will rob anyone who is not clever about business."

"Like Baumgartner?" Jamie said.

Gray Feather smiled for a moment. "That was an adventure, was it not?"

Jamie smiled back. He flapped his shirt, trying to catch a hint of breeze. "We showed old Uncle Harry, didn't we?"

Gray Feather's smile grew wide and he slapped Jamie on the back. "We conquered him, too!"

"We licked 'em all!" Jamie shouted, giving Gray Feather a mock punch with his fist.

In spite of the heat, the two boys jostled in the dust, laughing, trying to outmaneuver one another.

"Hey, boys, isn't it hot enough without you working up a lather?" said Pete putting a hand on each of their shoulders.

"We were just having some fun," Jamie protested.

"Well, Lord knows it's good to hear someone laugh," Ma said, "but I want you boys to wait to get your clothes changed before you start with the horseplay."

"Yes, Ma'am," Jamie and Gray Feather said in unison.

"Can we go swimmin', Ma?" Jamie pleaded.

"Well, I don't know. That river still has a swift current, even with no rain all summer. And James, you don't swim well."

"There's a shallow spot, where folks wade out to fetch water. It's only to our knees and moves slow as molasses," Jamie said.

"But I know you boys and you won't stay in that spot, you'll venture out." Ma said.

"Let them go, Anja. They deserve a little relief from this heat. I'm half tempted to go with them," Pete said.

He laughed when he saw the expression on Jamie's face.

"Just funnin', James. Your mother has plans for me, anyway."

"I want to be able to take a chair out on the porch to do my sewing where the light's better. If I tried to go out there now, I'd roll right off like an egg."

"I told your ma I'd brace it up and fix the rotten boards. Thought the Lord didn't want folks working on Sunday," Pete said, putting his arm around his wife's shoulders.

"Since you're at the mill twelve hours a day, six days a week, Sunday's the only day to get chores done. I'm sure the Lord will make an exception this once."

"What're you sewing, Ma?" Jamie asked, pulling once again at the tight collar of his shirt, hoping she would notice.

"Oh, I'm needing to make something special."

"Something special?

"Don't ask questions, James. Your ma's got some sewing to do. Leave it at that," Pete said, his tone taking a stern note.

"But—I only asked what . . ." stammered Jamie.

The Home Wind

"Oh, Pete, he'll find out sooner or later. Let's tell the boys now," Ma said.

"Tell us what, Ma?" Jamie looked from his ma to Pete to Gray Feather, who had a small smile.

"Well, James. I need to make some clothes big enough to fit me as I get, well, bigger."

"Bigger? I think you're getting smaller. You give too much food to us and don't take enough for yourself."

"I have plenty. I piece all day at the store. Mr. Mueller is very generous. Well, anyway, there's things besides eating that make a woman bigger."

Now Ma was talking in riddles.

She saw the confusion on his face. They had reached the house and Pete held her elbow while she went up the rickety stairs.

"Oh dear, this is so difficult," she said.

"Your ma's in a family way, boy," Pete said.

"Huh?" Of course she had a family. She had Jamie and Pete and Gray Feather.

"Didn't his Pa tell him anything?" Pete said.

"Oh, mercy, no! That would be indecent," Ma said.

"What's indecent?" The prospect of something indecent being discussed, on a Sunday no less, had Jamie all ears.

"Didn't you even have any farm animals or kittens that the boy might learn something from?" Pete said.

"I'm afraid not," Ma said.

"Your mother is with child," Gray Feather said simply.

"Like the chickens laying eggs," Ma added.

"But I thought the chickens had stopped laying. Besides, folks don't lay eggs, do they?"

Jamie said. His head spun with heat and confusion. Why

did everybody but he know the answer to this perplexing riddle. What did eggs have to do with sewing on the porch?

They entered the house and Ma sat at the table. She pulled Jamie over by the hand. "You're going to have a new brother or sister, James."

Jamie's ears burned as if pressed between two hot griddles. How could he be so thick? But, still, what did this have to do with sewing?

"You remember Mrs. Vogel, don't you son, in house forty-two," Ma continued, "how she seemed to swell up?"

"Yes, Ma'am."

"Then, she had a little babe in arms one day, a daughter, Sara, they named her."

"Sure, Ma. Are you gonna swell up too?"

"I'm afraid so. That's why I need bigger clothes. Now you boys go change into some old things and go take your swim. That's all you need to know for now."

"I'll see to that porch, Anja," Pete said, you go lie down and take a rest."

Jamie felt his mouth fall open. He never remembered Ma taking a mid-day rest.

"Your ma needs to get more rest now that she's...well, she just does. We all got to make sure she doesn't overdo," Pete said.

Jamie still felt strangely in the dark. First of all, he had to adjust to the idea of a new sibling. He didn't think much of the pinched red little face of Mrs. Vogel's baby. It shrieked like a banshee, and balled its hands into compact little fists that it flailed around in some kind of a fit. One time he had seen Mrs. Vogel put a shawl right over the babe and it got real quiet. Jamie was afraid at first that she had smothered it and was relieved when she took the shawl off and began to gently pat the baby on the back.

The second part of the mystery was why his ma was planning to swell up. He looked at Gray Feather as he pulled on a raggedy pair of trousers and a threadbare shirt.

"Tell me why my ma is going to swell up," Jamie commanded.

Gray Feather gave him a mischievous smile. "I will think about it."

The boys made their way down the loft ladder and exited noisily through the door.

"Watch those steps, boys," shouted Pete. "I got the bottom one tore off. And be careful at the river," he added.

"Yes sir." Jamie said. He turned to Gray Feather. "You've got to tell me," he persisted.

"Why?" chided Gray Feather.

It was Jamie's turn to smile. "I'll make you a deal. I'll race you to the river, and if I beat you, you tell me."

"And what if I win?" Gray Feather said.

"You name the reward," Jamie said.

"You will help me," Gray Feather said, his voice growing solemn.

"With what?"

"You will help me destroy Angus MacGregor."

"But . . . I." Jamie felt his throat turn to cotton.

"Let the race begin," announced Gray Feather.

Jamie stole a look at his friend before barking out the command, "Go!" The boys ran for all they were worth.

CHAPTER EIGHTEEN
The Bribe

Jamie was still digesting the information given him by Gray Feather. Ma would be carrying the baby inside her. It would grow and eventually come out. How it got there in the first place was something a man and his wife figured out. Jamie wondered what all the side-stepping and embarrassed looks were about. It seemed simple enough.

The race had been declared a tie and the boys decided that each had won, rather than lost. Therefore, Gray Feather had told Jamie about the baby and now Jamie must help Gray Feather with the unspeakable task that lay ahead.

The river glided over Jamie's legs. He sat on a boulder mid-stream and enjoyed the coolness. Gray Feather had gone out to the middle of the river, but the water was only to his waist.

"I have heard that many logs have been left to rot in this river," Gray Feather said.

"Yeah. Pete said that they were all jammed up by July 'cause the river shallowed out. He's worried that they will run out of logs to saw if the fall rains don't come," Jamie said.

"The scaler, the man who I help tally the logs, says he will be moving on soon," Gray Feather said.

Jamie waited, wondering why it mattered to Gray Feather. They would find other work for him at the mill. Meanwhile, Jamie was stuck in the company store loading wagons and sweeping the floor. Ma was right, though, it had special privileges: an occasional peppermint stick, a pound of flour that the family wasn't docked for. Sometimes the man who ran the store, Mr. Mueller, favored Jamie with a small, melting shard of ice from the ice shack. Jamie savored its delicious chill on his tongue.

"The scaler . . . his Ojibwa name is *Shuh shuh gah*," Gray Feather said, bringing Jamie back to the river.

"But, he's not an Indian is he? He doesn't look like one." Jamie said.

"He is like me, an Ojibwa mother and white father. His name means Blue Heron, because his eyes are blue. His mother lives on a Chippewa reservation. He will be returning there before winter to be with her and his people."

Jamie slid off his rock and eased his bottom onto the stream bed. Water cascaded around him.

"Blue Heron has told me he is certain my father is staying in the bunk house where the men without families live."

Jamie shivered. He had known Gray Feather would bring up the subject of Angus MacGregor.

"His logs were the last to make it in before the river became too low. He is waiting for settlement from the mill then he will move on."

Jamie stood, watching the water stream from his clothing. He was filled with dread. It was no good, this idea of Gray Feather killing his father. Jamie wanted to help his friend, but he would never be a part of murder. It was one thing to tell a little fib, or to doze off in church, but this was another matter altogether. Though Jamie was devoted to Gray Feather, he felt duty- bound to stop the madness that would land his friend in jail—or worse! And if Jamie were to help, well, first off it would destroy Ma, and that would be more than Jamie could stand.

"I have a plan, my friend, and I need your help," Gray Feather said.

Jamie jammed his hands into his pockets. He wriggled a thumb through a hole and stared at the water churning relentlessly around his shins. No matter what happens, Jamie thought, the river just keeps going.

"I can't help you kill anybody," Jamie muttered.

"I will not kill him," Gray Feather said, "but I will punish him."

Jamie shook his head and began walking out of the stream. "How?"

"By threatening to reveal him to the company who he betrays."

"Revealing what?"

"Blue Heron says that Angus MacGregor is stealing from the Tompkins-Watson Company—that's who he works for. He has claimed that there are two log marks to be tallied, one for the company and one for himself. MacGregor has offered Blue Heron a cut of the profits from the stolen logs."

"But won't Tompkins-Watson know that all the logs didn't get counted?"

"He will tell them that many logs got snagged because of the shallow water and never made it to the mill. MacGregor has actually sawed the ends off many of the company's logs and re-branded them. Blue Heron has a keen eye. He noticed that the logs were a little shorter and the false-branded end more freshly cut. When MacGregor knew he was discovered, he offered Blue Heron a bribe."

"Is he gonna take it—the bribe?" Jamie said.

"He told MacGregor that he would, but intended to report him to the sawmill boss. Then a plan came to him."

"What?"

"Blue Heron is offering the bribe to me, in a way, as a tool to serve me."

Though robbery was a lot better than murder, Jamie was not keen on being part of stealing some logging company's receipts from a whole season's work.

"Ma says that stealin's a sin," Jamie said.

"Oh, we will not steal his money, my friend. He will give it away, very willingly, to a worthy cause."

"You mean like to the orphans and widows?"

"Yes. That is what I mean," Gray Feather said. He followed Jamie out of the river. Jamie had more information to digest. The boys began walking toward home. A strong breeze dried their clothes quickly and swirled funnels of dust down the street. Jamie looked at the sky, searching for rain clouds that weren't there.

"This is why I need your help, James. You must be my witness when I confront Angus MacGregor and tell him I have discovered his scheme, and that I want a cut of the bribe he is offering Blue Heron."

"You would do that—take the bribe?" Jamie felt sweat breaking on his forehead. A blast of dust stung his eyes.

"I will take the bribe, not for myself, but for the Ojibwa."

"I don't understand. How will you do that?"

"It is simple. I will take the money that Angus MacGregor gives me and I will deliver it to the reservation to help those who live there, to help them continue their way of life."

"But isn't that stealing from the logging company?"

The boys were close to home. They paused under the shade of a tree.

"Remember, James, if someone steals your boots, you must take them back."

"Why must you always speak in riddles?" Jamie said. He was hot and impatient. "What has taking a bribe got to do with boots?"

"It is this way, James. The logs never belonged to the Tompkins-Watson Company or Angus MacGregor or to the sawmill. Those logs were stolen. Stolen, James, from the Ojibwa Indian Reservation."

"But how do you know?"

"Blue Heron told me. He was at the reservation last winter when Tompkins-Watson came and logged many trees. The government did nothing to stop them, though the law was being broken."

Jamie and Gray Feather moved toward the little house number 47. The porch was now straight. New boards, bright and clean were interspersed with old. Ma was on the porch plucking a chicken.

"Now do you understand, James, about taking back the boots?"

Jamie nodded. He guessed he understood. You can't steal what's rightfully yours. It was the same as getting the supplies and horses back that Uncle Harry had stolen back in Seney, wasn't it?

The Home Wind

"Can I count on you, my friend?" Gray Feather whispered. Ma looked up from her scrawny chicken and smiled. Jamie glanced at Gray Feather and gave a conspiring nod.

The stewed chicken was tough as shoe leather. Jamie finally resorted to swallowing a bite largely un-chewed. He gulped with the effort. Jamie glanced over at Gray Feather who seemed content with his meal. Gray Feather was always grateful for the food he ate and the tattered clothing he wore. He never complained, Jamie noticed, about hardships and injustices. Instead, he sought to make things right. Jamie wondered if all Indians were like that. Ma often said "Charlie" was a good Christian, never complaining and always at hand when he was needed. She had quickly added that James was a blessing, too, but for an Indian, Charlie was indeed special.

Since they had arrived at the Menominee mill town, Jamie had felt a distance growing between him and Gray Feather. He couldn't exactly figure it out, but Gray Feather had changed—seemed preoccupied. Maybe thinking about this man, Angus MacGregor, but Jamie thought there was more. For one thing, Gray Feather had stopped telling stories. "Perhaps later, my friend," he would tell Jamie. But later never came. Gray Feather talked of his time at the mill with Blue Heron, how the blue-eyed Indian spoke of the reservation and the people's struggle there. Gray Feather said that Blue Heron saved most of his earnings from the mill to buy food and supplies to help the reservation survive the winter. Sometimes Jamie was jealous of that friendship, though Blue Heron was a fully-grown man, perhaps eighteen or nineteen years old.

164

A knot twisted at Jamie's stomach. He felt—he knew he was losing his friend. But to what? It seemed when Gray Feather wasn't scheming to destroy his father, he was preoccupied with the Chippewa. Of course, Gray Feather always called them Ojibwa. He said that the name Chippewa was the white man's name, not his. What did it matter? Jamie wondered. Gray Feather was a part of his family now, wasn't he? Gray Feather turned his dollars over to Ma each pay day, but for a few coins. He sat at their table to eat, slept in the loft with Jamie as if they were brothers, and went to church with them. They accepted him as a part of the family, didn't they? Yet . . . did Gray Feather accept them?

Jamie rose from the table and carried his dishes to the wash tub. The water buckets to fill the tub were empty. Why hadn't they gotten water when they were at the river? Jamie picked up two of the buckets.

"I'm goin' for water, Ma."

"I will go with you," Gray Feather said, picking up two more buckets.

The wind had increased, swirling dust in the street and giving the air a murky look, like looking through a dirty window. The boys walked in silence. Jamie waded into the river and dipped a bucket into a pool, trying not to pick up too much sand.

"I can only get it half full. I'll keep filling the others with this bucket," Jamie said. Soon the buckets were nearly full and they boys began their trip back to the house. "When will we get the money?" Jamie asked.

"Blue Heron says that the money will change hands on Wednesday. We must move quickly, before MacGregor leaves town. There is a steamer coming a week from tomorrow. I am sure he will be on it."

The walk home was uphill and Jamie became slightly winded. They stopped under a dusty tree.

"It is too bad they did not leave more trees for shade," Gray Feather said, looking up at the pine's browning needles.

"This one was not cut because it is too puny. I think it will die, anyway," Jamie said. He cleared his throat. "How will we do it? Get the money, I mean."

"I believe MacGregor will visit the saloon after he gets payment. We will wait in the alley for him to leave the saloon. He will take the alley to the bunkhouse where he sleeps."

"But it will be late. What about Ma and Pete?"

"We will move silently, my friend, after they are asleep."

In spite of the oppressive heat, Jamie felt a cold hand grip his insides. This was much more frightening than anything he and Gray Feather had ever done. And something nagged at him, a voice, telling him it was wrong. We are just taking back the boots, he told himself. Jamie picked up his buckets and continued home, the hot wind lashing him. Gray Feather followed.

"And then what?" Jamie asked.

"I do not know what you are asking," Gray Feather said.

"How will you get the money to the reservation? Will Blue Heron take it with him when he leaves?"

Gray Feather craned his head to the sky. "This is all very strange," he said. "What's strange?"

"The birds. They are filling the sky."

"They do that this time every year, to fly south." Jamie was becoming annoyed. He wanted to know what Gray Feather was going to do with the money once they got it from MacGregor.

Gray Feather looked at Jamie. "But there are many different kinds of birds, all flying together. They are flying into one another. Look! One has fallen to the ground." Gray Feather set down his buckets and walked over to inspect the bird. "It is dead."

Jamie, too, looked at the bird. "Maybe it died from the heat."

"Perhaps," said Gray Feather doubtfully.

"When we get the money then do we give it to Blue Heron? Do you trust him?" Jamie persisted.

"Yes, I trust Blue Heron, but that is not my plan," Gray Feather said.

Once again, they had reached the steps of house number 47. Ma was out back surveying her withered garden. She had dug up a few gnarled potatoes.

"What is your plan," Jamie said, feeling a strange chill come over him as he stumbled into the house.

"I will take the money to the reservation myself," Gray Feather said. Jamie nearly dropped his water buckets. "But you can't!"

"I have to," said Gray Feather, pouring water into the wash tub. They had warmed some water over the outdoor fire that Ma had used to cook the chicken. It was out of the question to fire up the stove in the heat.

"But when...how? You'll come back soon—no! I'll go with you. No. Ma would never let me. Let Blue Heron take it. I'm sure you...he..." Jamie was frantically shoving dishes into the wash tub.

"Easy, Jamie. You will break everything," Gray Feather said, his voice gentle. "I will go when the time is right. Blue Heron will guide my way."

"What if he tries to rob you? You can't go. I'll get Pete to stop you. He'll stop you!"

The room was spinning. The hot room was squeezing the air from him, suffocating him. Gray Feather's face grew smaller and smaller in a frame of black. Jamie reached out to steady himself.

Jamie? Was the last word he heard before he felt the bones melt from his legs.

CHAPTER NINETEEN
Smoke

Caw! Caw! Caw! A racket penetrated the fog in Jamie's head. Something cold and wet lay on his forehead. It felt good.

Caw! Caw! Caw!

If only the crows would stop. Shoo! Away from the garden. But the garden had petered out long ago.

The sound of the crows was deafening. Something soft and gentle brushed across his face. A breeze, warm and soft as summer. Excited cawing broke through.

"I said shoo!" Jamie shouted, sitting up. A damp cloth fell from his forehead onto his lap. His head spun and he quickly lay back down.

"Easy, James," Ma said.

He was on the porch, lying on a blanket. Ma bent over him, fanning him with a tin plate. "Why are the crows so noisy?" he asked.

"We don't know, dear. They are frantic, though. How do you feel?"

"Okay, I guess. I... what happened?"

"It's the heat, Jamie. Here, have a drink of water." Ma lifted a ladle of water from a bucket. We think you just passed out from the heat. I pray to the Lord that you aren't coming down with something."

The Home Wind

"I'm fine, Ma," Jamie said. He sat up, slowly this time, and drank from the ladle. "Where's Pete and Gray Feather?"

"They went to the mill. News has it that the Lake Michigan steamer has docked in Menominee."

Jamie felt his heart skip a beat. The steamer! That would be the boat that Angus MacGregor would take when he settled up for Tompkins-Watson and filled the other pocket with the money from the stolen logs. That was unless Jamie and Gray Feather could convince him to turn it over to them under the threat of exposing him to his company. Waves of doubt rippled through him, making him shiver. Angus MacGregor would more likely cut their throats than turn over the money. What had Gray Feather gotten him into? A harebrained scheme, plain and simple.

Jamie looked around, blinking, trying to focus. The air was thick and hazy. The wind had died. He thought he smelled smoke.

"Is the peat bog flaring up again, Ma?"

"I suppose that could be it, James. Though, well, the smoke seems to be coming from the southwest, and the peat bog is east of here."

Jamie stood and walked out into the dusty yard. He sniffed the air. A faint whiff of smoke was in the air.

"You stay in the shade James Kangas. I don't want you going down, again, and bumping your head," Ma said. "I have some things to do and I can't keep an eye on you."

Jamie nodded and moved down the street, ignoring her instructions. The sawmill town seemed deserted. No ladies sitting on their porches. No children playing in the powdery dirt yards. Jamie peered down the street and saw no evidence of the men who usually gathered outside the company store to swap stories. Though his legs were a little wobbly, Jamie kept walking. Was he still dreaming? It was as if he were going through a ghost town. He saw movement ahead and squinted into the late-day sun. It was too big for a dog. As he approached, he realized that it was a deer walking down the middle of the street. It paused occasionally, drawing up a curled foreleg and sniffing the air. Was it sick? It seemed a little thin but otherwise showed no signs of illness. He watched, amazed, as the animal moved steadfastly down the middle of the deserted street toward the river. Maybe it was very thirsty, he thought. Perhaps all the other watering places had dried up.

Jamie continued toward the sawmill, hoping to find Pete and Gray Feather. Maybe the steamer wouldn't leave on Wednesday, as planned. Maybe Angus MacGregor would be stranded in town a few extra days, buying the boys time for a better plan. Jamie walked past a corral with two horses. They paced nervously within its confines, whinnying at Jamie as he went past. One pushed against the rickety boards of the fence. Jamie expected the nails would pop if the horse persisted.

"I don't have anything to feed you, if that's what you want," he said to the horses. Jamie noticed that there was hay in a wooden manger in the corral. Evidentially it wasn't food that the horses were concerned about.

Jamie soon realized where the men had gone. They were gathered at the sawmill. As he approached, he tried to find Pete and Gray Feather in the crowd.

The Home Wind

"I'm puttin' the missus and youngsters on that steamer when she leaves," he heard someone say.

"I heard it's the *Union* that's here and that she's goin' to be full up with lumber and pullin' a barge to boot. Ain't no place to put folks, 'cept those that already have passage."

"James!"

It was Gray Feather's voice, carrying through the din of the crowd. They spotted one another and Jamie hurried to meet his friend.

"Gray Feather! What's going on?"

"The steamer, *Union*, has docked. The captain has sent a messenger that they sailed through thick smoke. There's fire in Wisconsin."

Jamie struggled with the news. What did it mean? He knew Wisconsin was close by, but how close?

"There's talk of putting the women and children on the ship, in case the fire is coming this way," Gray Feather said.

Coming this way? Fire?

"Jamie. Gray Feather," Pete said, joining the boys. "We best head back to the house."

"What about the fire, Pete?" Jamie asked. "Is it coming this way?"

"Hard to say, son. Could."

They hurried down the street toward house number 47.

"Would you look at that," Pete said, pointing at a raccoon. They watched it waddle down the street within a few feet of themselves.

"He is going to the river," Gray Feather said.

"Should we go to the river? Will it be safe there, if the fire comes?" Jamie asked.

"Don't ask questions I can't answer. Sparks could start a fire anytime if that wind comes up."

They hurried up the porch. Ma had lit the lantern. An early darkness approached and the wind was picking up again.

They ate a tasteless supper of boiled potatoes by the light of the lantern. "The last of the potatoes," Ma said, poking at her food.

"How come it's so dark? It's only around six o'clock," Jamie said.

"It is the smoke, blocking the sun," Gray Feather said. His meal sat nearly untouched as did everyone's.

Jamie's eyes burned and his throat felt raw.

"What should we do, Pete?" Ma asked, looking at her husband. Wind rattled the windowpanes and pushed dust through the doorway.

"You and James be ready to head for the river. Gray Feather and I have to go to the mill and wait... in case. We'll take some blankets and sleep there. If a fire starts, foreman says he wants all the men on hand for a water brigade."

Jamie thought about protesting. Once again, he was left behind to hide in his ma's skirts. He knew Pete was in no mood for discussion, though, and kept his hurt and anger inside.

Jamie and Gray Feather started to carry the dishes to the wash tub. "Let's save our water," Ma said, "we may need it."

CHAPTER TWENTY
Fire!

The dawn came gray and angry through the loft window. Jamie had listened to the wind buffet the little house into the night as he lay awake. Finally, he dozed, only to awake to the strong smell of smoke, which burned his nose and throat. He wondered why Ma had not called him. Wasn't it time to go to the river?

He climbed down the ladder from the loft. Where was she? The curtain which hung over the doorway to her and Pete's bedroom was pulled across the doorway. "Ma...Ma you in there?" He shouted at the curtain. He listened for an answer but only heard the house creak and bang in the howling wind. Was she outside? Jamie stepped onto the porch into a gust of wind. Smoke and dirt swirled around him.

"Ma?" he called. He checked the outhouse. She was not there, either.

"MA!" he shouted, his voice carried off by the wind, "Ma, where are you?" Jamie stopped a moment and looked off to the west. The landscape was strangely illuminated, like the glow of the setting sun when it dips behind the trees.

Fire! Fire was coming. Where was she? Had she gone to the river without him? She would never leave him behind.

He raced into the house for one last look. She was standing in the doorway of the bedroom, clutching the door frame for support. The curtain had been torn from its nails and lay at her feet.

The Home Wind

"James...I," she whispered.

"Ma!" Jamie ran to her and tried to support her. "What's the matter, are you sick, did you fall?" he babbled.

"The baby, son. Too soon. Much too soon."

"What about the baby, Ma? What's too soon?"

"Don't ask questions now, James. You have to find Pete. OHHH," she moaned.

Jamie felt her weight as he tried to hold her up. He walked her to her bed and helped her lie down.

"I'll get Pete, Ma. You rest."

"Hurry, James!"

Jamie raced out of the house, leaping off the porch. Questions spun through him. Why would the baby come early, why would it come now, of all times? Gray Feather had told him it would be many more months. Jamie's legs pumped, muscles burning, in his race to find Pete. When he reached the mill he found chaos. Men flew about, gathering water in buckets and barrels and loading them in a wagon. A team of horses pranced and reared while two men tried to steady them and hitch them to the wagon. Other men were tossing water onto the mill and the stacks of lumber that surrounded it.

"Get it good and soaked," someone shouted, "that wind is bringing sparks with it!" Women and children were huddled on the riverbank. Some had blankets over their heads. Jamie plowed through the crowd shouting, "Pete! PETE!" He looked everywhere but could not find Pete or Gray Feather. He called their names over and over.

"They're gone."

Jamie spun around. Blue Heron!

"Where—where are they? Got to find Pete," Jamie panted, still winded from his sprint.

"Gone out of town to fight the fire. Keep it from coming in," said Blue Heron. "They will never stop it!"

"How far, how far? I've got to find Pete!"

"Too far. You better get to the river and stay put—"

But Jamie had bolted away before Blue Heron could finish. He had to get Ma to the river himself. No time to fetch Pete or explain to one of the other men. Jamie's eyes burned, tears stung his cheeks, blurring his vision.

"Oooof." Jamie had run into something, someone. He smelled a man's sweat, felt hands grasping his arms.

"Watch where yar goin' lad."

"Sorry," muttered Jamie, looking at the man's face. A jagged scar cut an irregular line through the man's red beard. Angus MacGregor! It had to be Gray Feather's father. Jamie had never seen him, but the scar was there as Gray Feather had said. No time for that now. Jamie wrenched free of the man's grasp, staggering from the effort, then rushed toward home. He looked over his shoulder for a moment, to see if MacGregor was watching him but the man was hurrying toward the men's bunkhouse. Strange, thought Jamie, willing his legs to go faster. Why isn't he helping fight the fire? Its glow was getting closer.

Jamie's ears roared with his pounding heart when he leapt onto the porch. Ma was inside, sitting at the table. Her breath came in gasps, as if she had been the one running. Her hair hung loose around her pale face. She was clutching her middle with one hand and the tea tin with the family savings in the other.

The Home Wind

"We've got to go to the river, Ma, the fire's comin'!"

"James! You were to bring Pete."

"He's gone to try to hold back the flames. Come on Ma, we've got to go."

Jamie grasped her hands and pulled her to her feet. The tea tin clattered to the floor.

"Got-to-take-our-money," she choked, coughing.

Plumes of smoke were curling through the windows and door. Jamie picked up the tea tin and reached for his ma just as her knees buckled from under her. The tin once again fell.

"Put— put the money in your pockets," Ma whispered.

"Can't, Ma, too many holes. We'll have to leave it." He looked frantically around the house.

"The stove!" Jamie said.

He went to the cast iron stove, opened the door and tossed the tin inside.

"We'll come back for it later, Ma, we've got to save ourselves!" he said, tugging her behind him.

"Can't." She grasped the doorway, legs wobbling.

"Ma!" Jamie watched her eyes roll and lids flutter. He slung one arm under her knees and the other behind her shoulder blades and lifted her. He staggered for a moment under the weight. He could do it, he told himself. It wasn't that far to the river. He paused on the porch, looking off to the south. The fire had progressed from a mysterious glow to angry flames moving steadily across the stump field, tinder-dry brush fueling its journey.

Jamie shifted his ma's weight for a better grasp. His legs felt oddly strong and steady, carrying them both down the street. He became aware of animals, wild and tame, running with him. Fox and rabbits fleeing in terror. Dogs, cats, deer, squirrels, all running for their lives. He went past the horse corral, the hay in the manger ablaze, flames licking the wooden slats. The gate was open, the horses gone, either turned loose to fend for themselves, or pressed into service for the fire brigade. Ma moaned and put her arms around Jamie's neck. It made her easier to carry.

"Pete? I knew you'd come," she mumbled.

Jamie did not contradict her. He concentrated on moving his legs: right left right left. His lungs burned with each smoke-filled breath. The river lay ahead; he could see it. He could see the mill and the men still throwing water on the piles of lumber. A grassy field next to the mill smoldered, charred paths zig zagging their way toward the mill. Sweat poured down Jamie's forehead. He wished he had a free hand to wipe it away. Only a little farther, he told himself, bearing under the sharp pain in his neck and back.

"Somebody help that boy and woman!" Hands rushed to help him. Ma was gently removed from his grasp. His arms seemed unattached, flopping to his sides.

"Why it's Anja Atkins. Did you carry her all the way, boy? Get her to the river."

Jamie followed numbly as his mother was carried to the river's edge and laid on a blanket. People were scrambling about, clutching a few personal belongings as they waded into the river.

"I want my baby doll," cried a little girl being carried into the water by her mother.

Jamie sprang to life. "She says the baby's comin' early!"

The Home Wind

"Oh Lordy, no," said a woman. "The doctor's gone. In case any of the men got burned trying to hold the fire back."

"Pete? Is Pete all right?" Ma had regained consciousness and rose on one elbow. "We don't know if anybody got hurt, missus, but heaven help us, she's goin'!"

Jamie was confused for a moment then turned to see what others were looking at. Sawdust piles around the mill had ignited, flames reaching for the walls of the mill.

"We need some water over here!"

Shouts and confusion followed while men tried to douse the fire, but the buckets of water scooped from the river did little to quell the growing flames. Soon the men were driven back by the heat, all but a few joining the women and children in the river.

"Get the Atkins woman into the boat."

Ma still clutched her middle as she was lifted into the boat. Another woman got in with her. Jamie couldn't remember her name. Jamie followed, walking out into the water alongside the boat.

"I wish I had some of my tea to stop the contractions," Ma said.

"There, dear. Just breathe deep," the woman said. "Better?"

"I—I think they've eased a bit, Martha."

"Good, good!" said the woman named Martha. "You're way to soon, Anja. Did this happen with the first one?"

"No," Ma said, looking at Jamie's anxious face. "How did I get here, James?"

"Why Anja, didn't you know that your boy carried you?" Martha said.

"The last thing I remember is standing at the doorway. James, you carried me all the way from the house?"

"Yes, Ma."

"Don't know that my Harold could carry me that far," said Martha, chuckling. "How's the pain, dear?"

"Better, Martha. Just a stitch now and then."

"Here now, hold this wet cloth over your nose to keep out the smoke," Martha said. They had found the deepest part of the river, the water at Jamie's waist. The river's current pulled at him in its unrelenting way. The world was coming to an end, yet the river pushed on.

Man thinks he can tame and control the wilderness, son, his pa had said. Jamie thought of the devastated land now shrouded in clouds of smoke, stump fields left in the wake of the loggers, the brushy tops left behind to fuel the wildfire. But the land will always reclaim itself. Jamie watched a chipmunk swim by. He hoped it would make it across the river to safety. Was there fire on the other side, too? Gray Feather had once told Jamie that the Ojibwa believe that to destroy the earth is to destroy ourselves.

It seemed to Jamie that these words of warning were coming to light. Surrounded by smoke, Jamie listened to the sound of the running river mixing with the crash of a building succumbing to the fire and the coughing and weeping of those whose lives teetered precariously around him. Ma and Martha did not speak, both huddled under a damp blanket.

Something strange approached Jamie, pink and round. As the object got closer, he discovered it was the snout of a small pig.

The Home Wind

"Look Ma, it's a pig!" Jamie said.

"Poor thing. It'll drown for sure," Ma said, peeking out from beneath her blanket.

Jamie reached over and cradled his arms under the pig, lifting it from the water. It snorted with labored breathing, legs thrashing the air.

"It's just a young one," Jamie said. "Easy there piggy, I won't let you sink."

As if understanding, the pig ceased paddling and turned a quivering snout toward its rescuer.

Suddenly there were shouts and a loud crash. They watched the mill collapse onto itself, flames roaring from the roof.

"Oh dear," Ma said, her voice wavering, "I wish Pete were here."

"Now, I'm sure he and my Harold are fine. They have plenty of water and wet blankets to get under if they need," Martha soothed.

Jamie's eyes stung with tears. He felt the hair singe on his head from burning ashes carried by the wind. Ma stretched a portion of her blanket toward Jamie.

A loud explosion shook the air, nearly causing Jamie to drop the pig.

"Dynamite! There goes the store!" someone shouted.

Fragments of wood rained down around Jamie, hissing as the flames were extinguished in the river. He stared in disbelief as an in-tact coffee grinder splash-landed, floated momentarily then sank into the current.

All the men had given up the fight and joined the women, children, and animals in the river. Jamie looked around at the spectacle of humanity and animals all clinging for life in the river. A rat riding a limb floated by. It twitched its nose at Jamie.

"Maybe he'll find a safe place to land," Jamie said to no one in particular.

It seemed hours that Jamie held the now not-so-little pig. It hung limply in his grasp, exhausted from its ordeal. The air had begun to cool. Jamie shivered, wet and cold. The wind was shifting back onto itself, allowing a view of the devastated town. Retreating black plumes wound thickly through the skeletal remains. Every structure had fallen victim to the fire, either reduced to a pile of ashes, or a few charred uprights. Stillness hung in the air as Jamie watched the smoke undulate and retreat through the ruins.

Martha and Ma came from beneath their blanket. Martha was making clicking noises with her tongue and Ma said nothing. Jamie knew what she was thinking because he was too. What about Pete and the other men who had gone to fight the fire? And Gray Feather! What had become of his friend? Jamie tried to swallow the hard lump in his throat. Surely they had found a way to survive. A few drops of rain began to fall.

All eyes shifted heavenward. Rain, precious rain. It grew steadier and stronger. Ma began to hum, then in a shaky voice, broke into the hymn "Breathe on me, Breath of God." Martha joined. Jamie's voice squeaked in accompaniment.

> Breathe on me, breath of God,
> fill me with life a-new,
> that I may love what thou dost love,
> and do what thou wouldst do.

The Home Wind

Soon the entire river of people was singing as if this were a Sunday service. Jamie wished he knew the words better, for never did a hymn seem so important.

The rain was coming down heavily. Folks worked their way toward shore, helping one another, rescuing animals. Smoke became steam rising from the town, the coals and ashes hissing in the rain.

> Breathe on me, breath of God,
> so shall I never die,
> but live with thee
> the perfect life of thine eternity.

"There, look!" someone shouted.

Through the smoke, Jamie could see a small band of figures approaching, working their way around the cinders and smoldering structures. The rain intensified, blinding Jamie as he moved toward shore.

"Pete?" Ma cried, clambering out of the boat, nearly capsizing it. Martha yelped, clutching the sides.

Jamie strained to see. Was Gray Feather there, and Pete? It was too hard to see. He must go find out. Jamie pushed through the water.

"Jamie, be careful!" Ma shouted after him. The pig squealed and squirmed in Jamie's grasp. He set it on shore and ran toward the returning group of fire fighters.

"Gray Feather! Pete!" he shouted, stumbling from the weight of his wet clothing. The pig shook itself and trotted after Jamie.

"Pete, Gray Feather?" he called again.

But no one answered his call.

CHAPTER TWENTY-ONE
The Home Wind

"Your man and the Indian went to look for you, Missus," said a soot-covered man. He held the ragged remains of a blanket. His clothing was filthy and half his beard was singed off.

"Where?" Ma asked.

"Back to your house, Ma'am. He was going to go by there, then high tail it to the river. Rest of us got cut off by a backfire and had to hunker down in a near dried-up pond. Buried ourselves in the muck, we did."

Jamie and his ma hurried toward house number 47 with the pig trotting dutifully behind. "Oh, Lord, why did he try to go to the house?" Ma fretted.

"Ma, slow down. You don't want to start having those pains again."

Jamie wanted to run, too, but his strength was gone. He staggered numbly, trying to support his mother.

"I'm certain the house is gone, James. Why didn't they come to the river?" She clutched her soggy skirts, heavy with mud and ashes. The rain continued and Jamie realized they would have no place to get warm and dry. He carried the sodden blanket that had sheltered them at the river and found its leaden weight strangely comforting.

The new steps Pete had built were just so many ashes; the outhouse and chicken coop indistinguishable. A few blackened uprights were the only evidence that a house had once stood where the gray ashes lay. That and the cast-iron stove and the stone rim of the well.

Ma buried her face in her hands and began to sob. Jamie tried to comfort her, but felt his own insides explode with grief for his lost friend, Gray Feather, and for Pete. They stood, hunched and sobbing. Ma was making a strange wailing noise Jamie had never heard, like a wolf almost. The haunting noise filled the air.

"Jamie, it's going to be all right, you're hysterical. You must stop that wailing," Ma said.

"I'm not wailing, Ma. I thought it was you."

They both lifted their heads to listen.

A muffled shout.

Ma and Jamie looked at one another.

"Where's that coming from?"

They looked around. The noise came again, weaker. The pig trotted to the well and sniffed at the base.

"The well. It sounds haunted!" said Jamie.

They rushed to the well. Jamie leaned against the stones then yelped. They were hot from the fire.

"Down here!"

Jamie draped the blanket over the hot stones and leaned against it to peer into the dark cavern of the well. Two sets of eyes stared up at him.

"Pete? Gray Feather!"

"Oh!" shouted Ma also leaning over the edge. "Pete! Charlie, you're alive"

"Darn near roasted to death," Pete shouted, coughing.

"We have the rope down here," Gray Feather said, his voice rasping like a saw. "I will toss it to you."

It took several tries, but eventually Jamie caught the rope and took up the slack.

Ma and Jamie heaved with all their might. Jamie shot a worried look at Ma, afraid the strain would start the pains again. But there was no other way. It took them both, heaving and straining, to finally pull Gray Feather from the well. Now there were three of them on the rope, making it easier to hoist Pete to the rim.

"Ouch! That's hot," shouted Pete, clutching the stone.

Ma and Pete fell into a tight embrace, creating a spectacle that made Jamie blush. He and Gray Feather grasped one another with more restraint. Both Pete and Gray Feather were missing their eyebrows and eyelashes giving them a comical, surprised look. Their singed hair sprung in curls from their heads.

"You look very strange," Jamie said, trying to suppress a snort of laughter.

"As do you, my friend," Gray Feather said, laughing. "What is this," he asked pointing at the pig.

"I saved him from drowning," Jamie said. "I guess he's ours, now."

"Looks like he's a she," Pete said, his voice heavy with exhaustion, "and she's about all we have left."

"Yes, the pig, this blanket and the clothes on our back, such as they are," Ma added. "Oh Pete, what will we do. All our hard work, our life savings gone! It's the same for everyone. None of us have a place to live!"

"No time to build, even if we had supplies," Pete added. "Only thing left is that old iron stove."

"The stove!" Jamie said. He rushed into the ruins of their house, mincing his way through the smoldering ashes.

The Home Wind

The others followed. Using his shirttail to protect his hand, Jamie jerked open the stove door. Inside sat the little tea tin, twisted from the heat.

"Oh, surely the money will have all burned up," Ma said, bending and looking inside the stove.

"What money? What in thunder are you talking about?" Pete asked.

Jamie retrieved the tin with a quick movement, burning his hand, and dropped it into the ashes. Jamie blew on his hand and shook his head doubtfully as he inspected the warped container.

"Is that our money tin?" asked Pete.

"The coins should still be okay," Ma said.

They pushed the tin onto a blanket. After it had cooled a few more minutes, Jamie wrenched off the lid, and reached inside. The bills felt slightly crinkly, but not scorched. It was all there, whole and spendable!

"Oh, Jamie," Ma shrilled, "Your brilliant idea worked! You've saved us."

"That your idea, son?" Pete bellowed, slapping Jamie on the back. Pete carefully picked up the money, folded it, slid it into a pocket then gave it a pat. "Good thinking, boy."

"He is almost as clever as an Ojibwa," Gray Feather added.

The pig grunted and rooted through the warm ashes. The rain had stopped falling. "Hello there!"

Everyone turned to watch a man approach.

"Everyone accounted for here?" the man asked.

"We're all alive, some a little singed is all," Pete said.

"That you under all that black, Joe?" Pete asked squinting at the soot-covered man.

"It is Blue Heron," Gray Feather said. "Joe is his white name."

"So far, only one lost to the fire," said Blue Heron. "That river saved our lives—that and the muck pond."

"And the dry well," Gray Feather said.

"Who died, Joe?" Pete asked.

"Found what was left of him in the bunkhouse ashes. Only one's not accounted for is that MacGregor fella."

Jamie looked at Gray Feather and watched his face turn stony.

"Why, in heavens name, didn't he go to the river?" Ma asked.

"Couldn't say, Missus. Some think he was going to see what he could pilfer from the men's belongings while they were all out fightin' the fire. Maybe he was drunk and passed out."

Jamie remembered how he had collided with MacGregor on his race to get Ma, then watched him go into the bunkhouse just as the fire was approaching town. He did not think the man was drunk and it would have been a perfect opportunity to steal. "Well, he got justice, then," Jamie blurted, without thinking.

"Now James, mind your tongue," Ma scolded. "Have some respect for the dead."

"We'll all be heading into Menominee tomorrow," Blue Heron said, "to see if there's some help there. Speculation is that with the wind shifting and the rain comin' when it did, Menominee might have been spared. Anyway, the steam ships should be there. Some folks will try to leave on those and go find kin to live with."

"My wife shouldn't make the trip on foot," Pete said.

"She's expectin'," Jamie blurted out.

"James!" Ma snapped.

Gray Feather chuckled and nudged Jamie. "You still have a lot to learn, my friend." Jamie's face flushed. Now what had he done wrong. He felt something bumping his leg.

The little pig looked up at him. Jamie squatted next to it and scratched it behind the ears. He didn't like the way everyone was looking at the little pig. Jamie was very hungry and he knew the others must be too. But it would be unthinkable turning this pig into supper. Jamie cradled his arms around the pig protectively.

"We've got some horses. Can she ride?" Blue Heron asked.

"Of course I can. I can walk, if need be. We can't say here," Ma said.

"That we can't, Missus," Blue Heron said. He tipped the tattered remains of his hat at her. "I will be on my way to finish checking on folks."

"Will you be going to Menominee, Joe?" asked Pete.

"For a while, then I'm going home for the winter. Back to the reservation. I worry that I have no money to take with me. It was sewn into my mattress. Just a pile of ashes, now. My people depend on my help to survive the winter."

Jamie saw Pete's hand move to his pocket and hesitate. "I suppose we can spare a few greenbacks," Pete said, looking at his wife. She smiled and nodded.

"I'd like to do more, you understand," Pete said,

pressing a wad of bills into Blue Heron's hand. "Got to think about my family."

Blue Heron smiled as he smoothed out the bills then folded him. He removed his battered hat and slid the bills into the lining.

"Should have put my money here to begin with," Blue Heron said, patting his hat. "I'm very grateful for this Pete, Missus. It will make a difference. I understand about taking care of one's family. I must go now." Blue Heron looked at Gray Feather. "You must decide soon. *Kee-way-din* calls to those who listen."

"Yes, *Shuh-shuh-gah*. I will decide soon," Gray Feather said.

Jamie looked at Gray Feather, who was looking at Blue Heron. Please don't go, too, Jamie pleaded silently. "Gray Feather, what is *Kee-way-din*?" he asked.

"The home wind," he whispered. "It is the wind that calls me home, my friend."

CHAPTER TWENTY-TWO
From the Ashes

Hunger had become a part of him. They had dug through a potato field looking for something to eat on their journey to Menominee. Jamie poked in the ashes and mud with his knife, only finding rocks. The pig—he had named her Cinder—was the most successful, rooting up an occasional tuber with her twitching snout. The potatoes were hard as stones and blackened, literally cooked in the ground. Jamie had tried to eat one, but it was inedible, even to a starving boy, and he tossed it back to Cinder. She seemed content to crunch the unlikely meal.

Exhaustion gripped the rag-tag group of survivors. Each had been robbed of sleep the night before, cold and wet and full of doubt. It seemed everyone had simply been waiting for daylight to begin their exodus to Menominee some seven miles away. Jamie expected the others were having the same thoughts as he, wondering what lie ahead. Would there be a Menominee? Had it been spared by the fire? Though they had started the trip as one large group, soon the band of people fragmented, the more robust taking the lead and those who were sick or injured, or with small children lagging behind.

The horse Ma had been riding staggered, stumbling often. There was no food for it, either, the grasses having all succumbed to the fire. Finally, Ma dismounted and led the animal. "It will do us no good to kill this horse," she had stated under Pete's protests. "We must find him something to eat."

Eventually they found some vegetation near the river that had survived the fire. The horse cropped the grasses and leaves greedily. Ma and Pete sat on the bank, along with Cinder, while Jamie and Gray Feather forged ahead. They had reached a stand of trees that had been spared by the axe, only to be blackened by the fire. The ground beneath the trees was scorched, ashes still holding a touch of warmth.

"Look to the ground, James. Perhaps we will find a dead rabbit or other animal to eat," Gray Feather said.

Jamie shuddered at the thought. "Shouldn't we just wait until we reach Menominee? There will be food there, I'm sure."

"If there is a Menominee." Gray Feather poked through the ashes with his foot. The sole of his boot flapped loosely.

"You need new boots," Jamie said, "I can see your toes sticking through."

Gray Feather nodded, continuing his search. "Yes, I will need new ones, before I begin my trip." He cast a glance at Jamie.

"Trip?" Jamie felt an old fear grip him. "You mean with Ma and Pete and me? Pete still says we're going to find us a place at Birch Creek, even though everything's probably burnt up there, the land will still be good for farming. Better, Pete says, since the fire. Still time to build a cabin before winter, and stock up..."

"That is where you will go, my friend."

"But you can go, too, Gray Feather! Angus MacGregor is dead. You are free, just as I am free from my *Mitchi Manitou*."

Jamie had felt strangely at peace with himself since the fire. He couldn't imagine how he had managed to carry his ma to the river. The preacher said maybe it was the Lord helping, or maybe it was his pa giving him a hand from his place in heaven.

"You know what I say, James?" Ma had said, "I say it was you, plain and simple, who saved my life. I am so blessed to have a son like you."

But why couldn't his friend, his brother, be at peace, too? The haunted wolf still lurked within the Indian. Why couldn't Gray Feather accept Jamie's family as they had accepted him? He had slept under their roof, eaten at their table, shared their joys and sorrows for so many months. That was being a family, wasn't it?

As if reading Jamie's thoughts, Gray Feather said: "I must go, James, because it would be too easy to be comfortable in your world. But I don't belong there."

"But you do. You do belong with us, we—we, well love you like..."

"Like one of your own?" Gray Feather turned to face Jamie. "Don't you understand, that I cannot accept being like someone? I must be true to who I am—what I am. Ojibwa. The white part of me died with Angus MacGregor. I will leave with Blue Heron to go to the reservation in Marquette."

Jamie did not try to hold back his tears; they splashed freely down his cheeks, dripping off his chin into the ashes.

The Home Wind

Gray Feather placed his hand on Jamie's shoulder. Jamie knew it was true, what Gray Feather was saying, he belonged somewhere. Jamie knew, too, that his friend deserved more than simple survival, which is all a white family could offer him. But would it be any better at the reservation that he had fled not that many months ago? It wasn't for these reasons that Jamie wanted Gray Feather to stay. Jamie admitted to himself that his reasons were selfish.

The boys stepped out of the charred woods into a clearing. Gray Feather jutted his chin high. "Perhaps I will someday win back that which was taken from my mother and all those like her."

Jamie nodded, chin to chest, watching his feet shuffle through the ashes. He sighed. How would he ever survive without Gray Feather showing him the way? Who would explain things, who would save him as he blundered along through life? Jamie's toe struck something: a piece of wood. Absently he lifted it and stared at it. If only he could carve away that which didn't belong, maybe the piece of limb would give him the answer. Jamie touched his fingers to the sheath that held his knife. It was well used now, the handle darkened with sweat and the blade showing signs of repeated sharpening.

"Look James! It's Menominee, just past that rise. The buildings are there . . . and it's green!"

Gray Feather turned to face Jamie, but he did not hear. Slowly Jamie pulled his knife blade across the wood. Blackened shavings floated around him. He worked faster, his hand flying with purpose. He remembered inspecting the firewood back at the lumber camp, looking for the vision—the spirit in the pine—that Gray Feather had told him lived there. But no matter how many pieces of wood he had looked at, they had withheld their secrets, as if angry with Jamie for the destruction he was a part of. But this humble piece of wood was different. It was giving him something. He carved madly, a blister rising on this thumb.

A trickle of sweat ran down Jamie's forehead while he labored, cutting away piece after piece as if his life depended on it. Jamie dropped to his knees, bracing the wood against his thighs. His hands, blackened by the charred wood, continued to work furiously. They felt as if they were no longer a part of him, but the hands of a puppet being pulled by invisible strings. Then it was all so clear, the answers flowing like water from the sluice gate. Just as Gray Feather would seek to right a wrong, so would Jamie. Somehow, the trees must all be replanted. But how? He looked into the wood and he saw a face. It was the face of his father. Had he carved that?

"Pa?"

A sudden breeze lifted the ashes at his feet, swirling them and carrying them away. Beneath lay a pinecone, remarkably untouched by the fire. *It starts with a simple pinecone, son.*

Jamie stooped to pick it up. He inspected it closely, marveling at how something so small, so insignificant could ever become a champion pine.

Jamie glanced at the wood sculpture which he still clutched in one hand. The face of his pa was gone; replaced by crude, random slash marks. He dropped the wood piece into the ashes. Carefully, deliberately, Jamie pushed the

The Home Wind

pinecone into his pocket and began walking. He would plant it when they reached their new beginning.

The Home Wind Discussion Guide

1. Gray Feather tells Jamie that it is not stealing to take back something that belongs to you. Do you agree with this? In chapter 11, "The Thief," describe what is stolen and how Jamie wrestles with his doubts about Gray Feather. But Gray Feather also talks about a person having something else stolen—something intangible. What is he talking about and is there is any way to regain such a loss?

2. Both Jamie and Gray Feather carry burdens. What are they? Are either of the boys able to lighten their burdens? How? Do you have any burdens you are carrying that you wish to "unload?" Think about how you might do this.

3. Gray Feather is the victim of a prejudiced world. What are some acts of bigotry and stereotyping that take place in the book? How does Jamie feel about the treatment of his friend? Are there other incidents of prejudice and stereo-typing in the book, besides toward Native Americans?

4. Describe the gender roles during this time period? Jamie is eager to become a man. What does Jamie believe it means to be a man? How is he conflicted about his feelings of resentment when required to do "women's work?" What is Gray Feather's perspective on coming of age?

5. Jamie is humiliated by Larry Flannigan in the chapter "An Eye for an Eye." Do you think it was wise of Jamie to seek revenge? Was his plan for revenge flawed? How so? And what was the outcome? How do you feel about playing a prank on someone? Can it be simply good fun among friends and family? When is it not funny?

6. Books often have past occurrences within the main story. This is called a backstory. What is Jamie and Ma's backstory? What is Gray Feather's? How were they necessary to understand the main story?

7. There have been times in history that environmental disasters have occurred due to people making horrible mistakes and poor decisions, such as The Dust Bowl and the Exxon Valdez oil spill. Has a similar situation occurred in the book? What was the cause and eventually the results of the treatment of the environment? Jamie often hears his deceased father's voice giving advice and making predictions. How did this affect Jamie's view of what the loggers were doing?

8. What is the meaning of good stewardship of the land? Have you done anything you consider to be an act of good stewardship?

Other suggested reading:

The Absolutely True Diary of a Part-Time Indian
    by Sherman Alexie

Lay That Trumpet in Our Hands
    by Susan Carol McCarthy

Out of the Dust
    by Karen Hesse

Yolanda's Genius
    by Carol Fenner

About the Author

Terri Martin has lived in Upper Michigan for over 20 years and in spite of the 250 plus inches of snowfall, has no desire to live anywhere else. *The Home Wind* is her second children's novel and is the result of much research about the logging era of the Upper Peninsula. Her first middle grade book, *A Family Trait*, was published in 1999. She also has a collection of humorous short stories published in 2020 entitled: *Church Lady Chronicles-Devilish Encounters*. Terri has a Masters' degree in creative writing and has a regular column in *UP Magazine*, featuring humorous short adventures involving unlikely characters who may be slightly off the grid in their thinking. A lover of the outdoors, Terri has also had feature articles published in several outdoor magazines and literary journals.

To contact the author or order books:
gnarlywoodspub@gmail.com

Breath on Me, Breath of God
Words: Edwin Hatch, 1878
Music: Robert Jackson, 1888